T0062973

Ghost of Passion

BY HABIBAT ONYIOZA SHEIDU

Order this book online at www.trafford.com
or email orders@trafford.com

Most Trafford titles are also available at major online book retailers.

Print information available on the last page.

ISBN: 978-1-4269-1841-4 (sc)

Trafford rev. 12/17/2016

www.trafford.com
North America & international
toll-free: 1 888 232 4444 (USA & Canada)
fax: 812 355 4082

Dedicated to my beloved dad, Saka Uru Sheidu for always encouraging me to write.

Acknowledgements

I appreciate these special people for their contributions and encouragement:

Chinwe Onuoha, Halima Onozare Sheidu, Remy Olagunju, Kelechi Chikwendu, Elizabeth Obaje, Fatima Bagudu, and Temilolu Oluwakemi Okeowo, Esther Tuebi Ateboh, Kunle Ogundele, Kunle Lawal, Muhammed Adamu Danjuma, Fatima Anako, Oyiza Anako, Mukhtar Bakare

Chapter 1

A T MY AGE people wonder how I gather the strength to keep punching my keyboard.

"What's your grandfather always doing on the computer?" I would hear people ask my grandchildren. Scribbling it out with my hands, would be easier... but this is so important to me that I dare not allow anyone read it until I am through. You can't imagine what people around me would do just to catch a glimpse. It's really tough hiding it from them because they love me so much. The kind of love they have for me is so obvious. I can smell it, see it, and can even touch it... But, lately their excessive display of affection is suffocating me a kind of situation that will make you want to scream and call the police. My privacy has long been taken away from me because whenever I walk out of my bedroom someone walks in and ransacks my belongings. Of course they don't know that I know what they do behind my back but in order not to break their hearts I feign ignorance. They read my diary everyday so I write what I'm sure they would want to read; mostly about how much I love them. My computer is not left out; they open all files I save so my hard disk cannot save any secrets.

"What about saving with a password?" I can hear you ask. Anything I save with a password would rouse so much suspicion that a swarm of bees would gather over my head, hovering patiently waiting for me to make a move then bam! They would sting. I've gotten you confused there right? Actually, my children and grandchildren are the bees, and the ones I told you are trying to kill me with love. They would not go anywhere until I open whatever it is that I saved with a password. One afternoon, I eaves dropped as my granddaughter was on the phone.

"...I tried to open the file but it was saved with a password..."

"I tried different passwords that I felt he could use but..."

"Alright, he's okay. It's just that he is pensive these days and spends too much time on the computer..."

"...Tomorrow? Alright, we'll be expecting you all" I felt like running away, all of them tomorrow? That phrase 'You all' was bad news because I knew what 'you all' meant. 'You all' meant a whole swarm of bees, a bunch of busybodies. I quickly went to the lavatory as my stomach started throbbing. I was also sweating and salivating. My parasympathetic nerve had obviously been stimulated by the sad news. When I came out of the lavatory, Sheena my granddaughter was right in front of me.

"Grandpa, should I call the doctor? I was passing by and heard your intestines rumbling"

"Thank you very much, I think I am fine now, my stomach decided to run and I guess it's through with the race."

"Really? But papa, running stomach is an indication that there might be something wrong somewhere"

"I had no idea Sheena, but tell me, what could be wrong with me my dear microbiologist".

"Firstly, it could be food poisoning caused by *Entamoeba histolytica*, of course, it cannot be botulism. Grandpa, the microorganism *Clostridium botulinium* has the ability to kill within a very short period of time".

"Wow, this sound interesting, Sheena why don't we sit down and talk more about these food poisoning microorganisms" Sheena loved discussing anything that had to do with her profession and she could spend hours telling you about a particular microorganism.

"Grandpa where did we stop?"

"You were telling me about the very deadly one" I replied.

"Yes, Botulism! This bacterium is gram-positive, rod-shaped and anaerobic. It is widely distributed in soils around the world..."

"How then does it cause food poisoning I know we plant our food crops on soils but we definitely do not eat soil"

"Yes grandpa, the name botulism actually comes from the Latin word for sausage and was chosen since the earliest recognized traces of botulism occurred in people who ate contaminated sausage. However many other food items have been sources of this food poisoning"

"Give me some examples," I demanded.

"Some of them are vegetables, fruits, meat and of course canned food," she added rolling her eyes. "In USA, canned foods have been implicated most of the time..."

"I think that's rational, you said the organism is anaerobic, meaning it would definitely grow inside containers that are sealed" She clapped for me.

"Grandpa you are wonderful, you are so brilliant"

"Come on, don't flatter me," I replied smiling broadly to be sincere I was truly pleased with myself.

"Now tell me how they are able to kill so easily" I resumed the conversation.

"Actually grandpa, there are a lot of clostridia species and *Clostridium botulinum*, just like any of them form endospores which may be unusually resistant to heat and can thus persist in food stuff despite cooking and canning processes. Under anaerobic condition these spores germinate. Growth of the bacteria may result in the release of a powerful toxin into the food. When someone eats the contaminated food, the toxin is absorbed into the blood stream where it may continue to circulate for as long as three weeks. The circulating toxin is carried to the various nerves in the body where it acts by blocking transmissions at the ganglia"

"Transmission at the ganglia?"

"Yes grandpa"

"That's strange please simplify it"

"Transmission at the ganglia simply means passage of signals through the nerve terminals. Blockade of transmission to the muscle produces paralysis within twelve to thirty six hours after ingestion of the toxin-containing food".

"What other symptoms could indicate that one has botulism?" I inquired

"Others are blurred vision and diplopia"

"Diplopia? What does that mean?"

"Grandpa, diplopia is simply double vision"

"Okay, go on my dear and please don't use those difficult scientific terms anymore".

"Alright grandpa, the visual disturbance is the first indication of paralysis. All muscles may be affected but respiratory paralysis is the most common cause of death which occurs despite treatment".

"Oh my God, it is so deadly" I replied

"Grandpa, it is so deadly that a few milligrams of it is sufficient to decimate an entire village".

"Hmm" I replied deep in thought this bacterium-*Clostridium botulinum* sure is deadly.

I enjoyed talking to Sheena, exploring her world of microorganisms was something really exciting and educative considering the fact that the organisms were invisible.

"So grandpa," she said cutting into my thoughts, "how are you feeling now?"

"As you can see I am fine. If I am suffering from food poisoning I guess I would not have sat down here for the past thirty minutes discussing with you without feeling the urge you know…"

"You are right grandpa" she replied. "But I'll like to take samples of your stool and urine tomorrow and if possible your blood, so that I could run some tests".

"Oh Sheena you don't have to worry I am perfect"

"No grandpa, I am not saying that anything is wrong with you, I just want to see your state of health that's all".

"Alright, prevention is better than cure, you will have the sample first thing tomorrow morning",

"Thanks grandpa" she said, hugging me tightly.

"Come on, I should be thanking you for all the trouble you'll go through" I replied.

"I guess I'll go and prepare dinner now". After she left, reality dawned on me.

"They are coming tomorrow," I told myself. I quickly got a diskette and copied out all the information. I saved the file as 'life' but I changed the contents to the names of all my children and grandchildren, their ages, occupation, and religion. At the end, I asked myself who I loved most and answered that I love all of them equally. The next day they started arriving one after the other. I had to collect lots of gifts as each of them came with a gift while those trying to impress me came with two. They pretended that it was a coincidence that they all came on the same day but they were definitely not fooling me.

"Oyiza!" Enesi shouted as she made her entry, a triumphant entry I thought, but unlike Jesus Christ that made his triumphant entry on an ass, Oyiza made hers with three suit cases, what on earth was she doing in my house with three suitcases? She would definitely not leave her husband and children to come and fuss over me...

"Enesi thank you very much," she hissed at him, as he was trying to help her with her suitcases.

"What have I done wrong big sister?" he asked

"Tell me that you didn't get the message I sent to you last week"

"Oh... Oyiza let me explain...."

"Papa" she screamed rushing forward to hug me, I felt as though a big bee was hovering and about to sting me. Running was my best option but I didn't want to appear mad because the last time they all came calling like this I was called a mad man. Anyway, I didn't run. I just closed my eyes and suffered the sting, she stung so hard that I could not breathe then she left me and started buzzing about how she missed me, she led me to her first suitcase and brought out her own present.

"Come on daddy open it," she urged...

After dinner they all gathered around me.

"So grandpa how are you doing?" Dele asked

"How does it look like I'm doing" I replied

"Come on grandpa," he said obviously hurt by my outburst, "I'm talking about your back does it still hurt?"

"Of course It does", I replied. "What do you expect from the muscles and joints of a ninety six year old?" They all laughed at Dele. Dele my grandson was a medical doctor. Halima, my grand-daughter cut in,

"Grandpa what about your computer?"

"My computer?"

"Yes grandpa, I mean are you enjoying working with it?"

"Of course" I replied "ask Sheena and Kemi they'll tell you how many hours I spend on the system"

"Kemi, how many hours does he spend?" asked Tayo. Kemi is Tayo's younger sister and Dele is their eldest brother they are the seeds of my daughter Ohunene who got married to the most gentle guy I have ever seen on the face of the earth_ Bayo Balogun. Bayo Balogun was a cultured gentle man with a capital G. The five of them came... No they were actually seven, Dele came with Doshima his fiancée, and Doshima came with Teso her brother, Teso came with his cat. At the end they got to the main purpose of their visit. My son Enesi went to the computer and came back to tell me that he wanted to go through a particular file but it was saved with a password.

"Daddy what's the password?" he inquired whispering into my ears.

"Come on, I replied. "That file is a secret one, I don't want anyone going through it"

"But daddy, you are not to keep any secret from me, you are old and anything can happen"

"Anything like what?" I asked. "Oh, let me guess, anything like my death right?" He kept quiet then continued gently.

"Daddy lets face it, if something like that happens the file would be lost forever and that would really break our hearts...."

"All right Enesi, the password is life but there's really nothing serious there..." Before I could finish he was back to the computer. I smiled happily at myself for a job well done.

When it was time for me to go to bed, I had to suffer their 'stings' once more, as everyone had to hug me goodnight. Enesi and Bayo saw me to my bedroom, tucked me in bed then said goodnight to me, just as the door shut behind them and I heaved a sigh of relief, the door was swung back open.

"Em papa" said Enesi "I will come and spend the night with you"

"What!" I exclaimed. "Bayo did you hear that? Enesi wants to spend the night with me".

"I don't see anything wrong with that sir" he replied.

"What is wrong with it is that Enesi has a wife and he came with her. Please leave me alone, go and sleep with your wife" Enesi and Bayo laughed hysterically.

"Who told you that she has not had enough of me?" Enesi asked.

"Enough? Who told you that they can ever have enough? Women, Forget them, they can never have enough of a man!" The two men fell on top of each other laughing at that.

"I'm sure you guys won't understand now but take my advice make it a point of duty to sleep with your wives every night and if possible during the day...." They kept laughing.

"And please if you guys don't mind I want to have my sleep"

"Goodnight papa" they chorused still laughing.

Finally, I had peace. I could not sleep but I had to pretend that I was asleep since my door was open; anyone could just walk in and you can imagine what would happen if I'm seen doing anything other than sleep. I'm sure you are wondering why I can't lock my door. The answer is very funny; they have this feeling that I would commit suicide so the key to my door was taken away from me.

A psychologist actually caused this misconception. She told them that I had suicidal tendencies when I was actually suffering from a kind of drug interaction that happened one morning. I woke up with a splitting headache and back ache; the pain in my back was so severe that I decided to take three different drugs but before I knew it I passed out. I knew I passed out because the self-medication led either to over dosage or some kind of drug-drug interaction but my mistake was seen as a suicidal attempt. They believed that I wanted to take away my precious life because the shrink told them that I was very depressed, and that most suicides were as a result of depression. They assumed that I was depressed as a result of my wife's death but how wrong they were because I was not depressed at all. In my lifetime I've come to accept death as something inevitable. Why should we bother about a departed soul when our God is a God of the living and not of the dead? After all, our Lord Jesus Christ said 'Let the dead bury the dead'. They loved their mum very much, I loved her too but it was like a replay of something that had happened to me before even though the circumstances were different.

Why my wife's death wasn't really a big deal to me was because I had seen a number of my loved ones walk through the valleys of the shadow of death.

What have I not seen in my ninety-six years of life? My children misunderstood me completely. It's not their fault anyway, it's just because for the past sixty-two years I've lived a lie... My pensive mood wasn't depression at all. I was always silent because I was thinking deeply about the past, the present and the future. My past which none of my present family knew about, my present which none of my siblings and past family know about, and my future which I myself know nothing about. Yes, my wife's death seriously affected me. It got me thinking about my first wife, my children, my best friend, my sisters, my nephews and nieces. I longed to see them. Oh God, it hurts me, it's an agony...

All these thoughts led me to write this story. I have kept secrets but now I want the whole world to know the real me. Yes I want every living soul to hear about my life perhaps Yvonne or

Mac would read this story... The possibility of their being dead is something I can never accept. I had to see Mac again even if just for once, oh God please I have to see Mac again...After my 'suicidal attempt', the whole family gathered around me and pleaded with me not to take my life.

"Papa", said Enesi. "We know you want to be with your sweet heart but please papa we need you too, papa please don't leave us now" It was funny. How was he so sure that Ahuoiza and I would be in the same place after death? Oyiza cut into my thoughts.

"Papa from now hence forth we are going to be there for you, we'll make sure that you are not lonely. Sheena and kemi are going to be living with you and we'll visit you always"

"Yes papa" said Ohunene. "Anything you want you shall get and...."

"Anything?" I cut her short.

"Yes papa, anything you want, is there anything you need right now?"

"Yes" I replied. They were all surprised probably they thought I was going to ask for another wife!

"I need a computer," I said. They all laughed, Eliza started talking.

"Papa, what do you need a computer for?"

"I want to write a book" I replied

"A book?" they all chorused

"About what?" Enesi asked

"My memoir" I replied. Halima my first grand daughter who refused to give me a great-grandchild enthused "you don't need a computer to write all you need is a writer..."

"Yes" cut in her cute younger brother Suliman who fulfilled my dreams by passing his elder sister and producing my first great grandchildren-the twins.

"Papa I am a writer, all you need to do is tell me the story and I'll write it for you".

"I am also a writer" I replied

"A writer?" They all chorused

"Yes" I replied, "I was one of the best writers when I was at the University"

"Daddy what University are you talking about. You never went to any University".

"My God", said Tayo "he has really lost it"

"Lost what?" replied her mum Ohunene. "Don't you see" Tayo continued. "He is completely insane,, I mean someone who's never attended lectures in a university..."

"Shut up" cut in her dad Bayo, "Do you know if he worked as a mechanic at the university? Please allow him bare his mind to us, so papa what were you writing about at the university?" he asked me.

"I was actually in the press club and at that time I was a student".

"What were you studying?" said Tayo giggling. "I studied Business administration. I even got my doctorate degree". At this they could not suppress it anymore; they all burst out laughing

"Actually" I continued, I wanted to study civil engineering but my dad wanted business administration because of his company so I changed my course... I didn't want to disobey and depress him, I was his only son and..."

"Grandpa calm down" Dele cut in, "it's okay, I'll give you the drug now".

"What drug?" they all asked?" I became scared. I hated the name Dele. I guess that's why I never got to like my grandson Dele the medical Doctor. When his parents named him Dele I protested but of course I could not change a name his parents adored. I gave him a pet name Eneji, and called him Eneji until he was six years old. One day, they came visiting and I called out to him.

"Eneji, come over here and give grandpa a hand shake," Instead of running down as usual he walked sullenly frowning his face.

"What is wrong with you, are you not happy to see grandpa?" Inquired his mum

"My name is not Eneji, my name is Dele," he said.

"Come on, Eneji is a pet name that grandpa calls you" Ahuoiza said trying to pat him on the head.

"Leave me alone" he shouted at Ahuoiza his grandma... His mum became so furious.

"Dele, apologize to mama immediately, how dare you talk to her like that?"

"Sorry grandma but I don't want you to ever call me Eneji, my name is Dele" then he ran off.

I felt stupid and rejected but that day I decided never to call his name. This kept us miles apart and I enjoyed the distance, I disliked all the memories his name brought back to me... Dele was my nightmare. He took away everything from me...

"This injection" Dele continued. "Is to calm mania, it will send him to sleep".

"What kind of mania? Who told you that he's manic?" Replied his father

"He's just depressed that's all" Tayo cut in,

"He is insane; he's talking about his father who died while he was two years old as wanting him to read business administration..."

They were all arguing amongst themselves. Some wanted Dele to administer the drug and some didn't. I became confused, as I certainly didn't want to be treated like a mad person. I started urinating right there so I excused myself. They continued arguing.

"See how he's urinating on the sofa, he has lost his senses..." "Come on he excused himself..." I closed the door behind me and tears ran down my cheeks. How sad. I realized that no one was going to believe me. If I insisted on the truth they would start giving me antipsychotic drugs so I decided to pull a trick on all of them. When I got back from the lavatory they were all quiet, obviously they had made their decision. Oyiza broke the silence.

"So papa you really want to write an autobiography?" I nodded.

"Do you know", she continued, "that in this country only ten percent of the population read books? If you want the whole world to know your story the aim will be defeated".

"But Mummy a lot of people watch movies, maybe he should write a script"

"Yes," said Halima "a movie will be better..." I laughed out loud and they were all flummoxed.

"So you all believe me? What can I write?" I asked still laughing_... they all joined me in laughter.

"Papa you will never change" said Rita my grand child

"I only pulled your legs; actually, I am so bored these days. A computer would do me good especially if I am hooked to the Internet"

"You are right papa, a computer you shall get first thing tomorrow morning"

That was how I got my PC. I am sure you now understand why my story is a guarded secret. From the information I gathered, I decided to write this script and make a Nollywood movie! But wait a minute from where do I start...? From the very beginning I guess.

Chapter 2

I INTEND TO OPEN this chapter from the very depths of my heart and the very beginning of my life.

In Anatomy the beginning of life goes way back to the very moment a sperm fertilized an egg and they both fuse then start meiotic division. After meiotic division, folding occurs then organogenesis and growth continues in the womb as the baby gets nourished through the placenta. If you expect me to start telling you about my life from there, then you'll be disappointed because I do not know the details of the beginning of my life. I am not a dullard, but sincerely I do not remember my childhood from age zero to five, it was as if I had no memory then, probably my memory store mechanism-the long term memory did not develop on time. My childhood wasn't really spectacular but I guess I developed a great part of my character then. I was very close to my dad who was a very rich man; at least that's what I told my teacher when she asked me what my father's profession was. My teacher was furious. She thought I was being silly so she pulled my ear. I was shocked at the length my ear could stretch since no one had ever done that to me before. It was thrilling and not painful at all. She asked me to tell her his real profession first thing the next morning. When my father got home that day I did ask him a lot of questions.

"Daddy is the ear made of rubber"

"Of course not" he replied, "what made you think so?"

I explained how my ear extended when my teacher pulled it and he laughed.

"Hey, Tom you are exaggerating but why did your teacher pull your ear

"Because I did not know your profession"

"You don't know my profession?"

"Of course I know dad"

"Then what's my profession?"

"You are a rich man" I answered

"Hey Tom, you can't be serious you mean you don't know my profession?"

"Are you not a rich man?"

"Yes Tom, I am a rich man and I am not just rich I am very, very rich" he said obviously pleased with himself "but" he continued, "what I do is different from what I am, and what I do is my profession"

"But daddy what do you do?"

"I am the manager of the company" he replied.

"What do you actually do?"

"I oversee everything"

"How do you oversee everything?"

"How do I oversee everything? Now how do I explain that to you, let me see... I manage the company's affairs, staff, money and many other things. So you tell your teacher tomorrow that your daddy is a business man okay?" I became confused.

"But daddy you just told me that you are a manager and now you're telling me that you are a businessman"

"Yes my son, I am a manager. A manager is also a business man".

"Then what do I tell my teacher?"

"My son, tell your teacher that I am a businessman".

I didn't get to understand my father's profession after all but my mum was a Nurse at least what she did was not that complex; she took care of the sick. Most Saturdays she would take me to the hospital with her...I loved the way the nurses dressed as they looked like angels in their white nursing uniform. I had two sisters, Happiness and Yvonne; Happy my elder sister was always unhappy and moody. She was actually about ten years older than I because after her, my mum had several miscarriages. This created a problem in the family because my dad saw the miscarriages as her fault. You can imagine the frustration my dad went through for ten years without having another child. My mum would get pregnant, they would carry out all the necessary precautions but within a few months she would have a miscarriage. Had my dad not been a 'devoted Christian' he would have married another wife. They tried different specialist hospitals before she finally had me. My dedication service was very grand and it was done with a special thanksgiving. I was named Thomas as my parents nearly doubted God when their prayer for another child was not answered immediately. After me it took another nine years before my younger sister was born. I can still remember the series of miscarriages my mum had before she finally gave birth to Yvonne. That period of nine years wasn't pleasant at all. My mum and my dad were always at each other's throat as daddy insisted that her recurrent miscarriages were as a result of her job. He asked her to resign but she would not hear of it. Yes, my dad had always wanted an educated wife but never did he think of marrying a woman who would spend most of her nights in the hospital. After their marriage my dad wanted to open a maternity home for her but she declined the offer on the grounds that she hadn't had enough experience, she promised to quit work immediately she acquired all the necessary skills. After ten years of marriage she had still not gathered enough experience. Ten years became fifteen years then twenty years. It became obvious that she would never leave the hospital because she was so attached to it...

I can still remember an incidence that happened in my final year in primary school. It was a Sunday evening; my dad and I went to the Donald's after lunch. We got back home in high spirits.

"Darling we are home" he called out to my mum but the maid answered us.

"Welcome sir" she greeted.

"Thank you Chioma and where's madam?"

"She went to the hospital..."

"Hospital...What happened? Was she bleeding?" My dad inquired

"No sir, she wasn't, she said it's an emergency". Happy came in and gave us the proper story.

"Daddy she's on night duty today, there was an emergency and she was called, she'll be back by five in the morning" My dad became furious, he picked the phone and called the hospital.

"Hello, can I speak to Mrs. Davies please..."

"Alright" my dad replied and started pacing up and down the room waiting for her to be connected.

"Hello", he continued, "Yes thank you..."

"Did you tell me that you were going to the hospital today?" yelled my dad

"Yes, sorry for disturbing you, Happy told me that it was an emergency but I want to know if an emergency is better than the baby..."

"Yes, if you say so, I am more concerned about the baby than you, I feel you want another miscarriage and God help you if anything happens to the baby".

He banged the phone.

"That was too hard on her dad" cut in Happy. "You know she doesn't want another miscarriage..."

"Will you shut up?" he yelled at Happy.

"Your food is on the table Sir"

"I said shut up" he yelled at Chioma then left angrily. I was about to go after him when Happy stopped me.

"Come here young man. Now go and eat" Chioma said dragging me by the collar into the dinning room. I wasn't hungry but I had to eat to please them else they would make the day miserable for me. Immediately they turned their backs I threw the food into the dustbin and pretended to be through. When I took the plate to the Kitchen, they were amazed.

"Tommy are you sure you're through?" asked Chioma.

"Yes"

"Come here Tom" said Happy, "better tell me what you did with the food"

"I said I ate it"

"Alright go, just get out of here"

I left hurriedly and rushed to find my dad. He was sitting on his bed and was looking so tensed up. As I stood by the door watching him, I felt very sorry for him and hated my mum. I could not just understand why she kept making him unhappy.

The ball I was holding fell from my hands so my dad asked.

"Who is there?" I was afraid of answering because I knew how angry he was.

"Tom is it you?"

"How did you know?" I said coming out of my hiding place.

"How would I not know" he replied grabbing me. Talking with my dad was one luxury I enjoyed.

"Daddy why don't you stop mummy from working since it annoys you?"

"No Tom, her job does not annoy me.. but, it's always annoying when she leaves like this. I've always wanted to have many children"

"Like how many?"

"Like ten or twelve" he replied "but each time she gets pregnant she overworks herself and miscarries".

"No dad, you can't blame her, if God wants the baby born I'm sure nothing can kill him, not even overwork," My dad laughed.

"Who told you that?"

"Pastor. He said God's will can never be changed"

"It's true, but Tommy God wants us to do the right things always. It's not just enough to have faith because faith without doing the right thing is useless. God didn't make any baby to be miscarried…"

My dad helped me develop my boldness. He always gave me the opportunity to express myself about anything; he would listen attentively as if I was making sense, laugh afterwards then state his own point. Periods when my mum was absent were always lovely for me as it afforded me the opportunity of spending time with my dad. After our talks we would go to my room and sleep together on my tiny bed. I guess he hated sleeping in his room alone when my mum was not there. In the morning, we would get set, eat breakfast then he would drop me in school himself.

That afternoon, I got home and met my mum

"Tommy, how are you? How was school today?" she inquired, not lifting her eyes from the magazine that she was reading.

"Fine" I replied.

"Go to the dining room and you'll find your food right on the table okay?"

"Alright mum" After eating I came back but she was still engrossed in her reading obviously a fashion magazine.

"Mummy where is Happy?" I asked

"She went out I guess"

"Out where mum?"

"I don't know, probably she went to the library"

"During holidays?"

"Yes Tom, Happy reads all the time, University is not like primary school you know"

"Mummy, why don't you want us to have brothers and sisters?"

"Who said that I don't want you to have siblings?" she said flipping through the pages of another magazine. "I'm sure your dad told you that"

"Not really" I replied. "Daddy said that you overwork yourself. Mummy must you work?"

"Yes Tom, I'm not a dummy so I must work"

"But daddy said you could have a place of your own where no one would call you for night duties"

"Tommy, go and do your homework okay, I want to finish this magazine"

"But mummy we're discussing something serious"

"Look Tom when your dad comes back, tell him that you guys cannot intimidate me"

"Intimidate? Mummy what's the meaning of intimidate?"

"Tom go and check it in the dictionary"

"Mummy please…"

"Tom leave me alone" she yelled. "Can't you see that I am busy?"

"But mummy can't you ever create time for us, if you're not busy at home you're busy at the hospital you don't even care about us"

"Excuse me, am I hearing you right? Tom are you having fever?"

"No mum I am not feverish, may be you are the one having fever". I replied defiantly

"Now Tom" she said pointing to the door,

"Get out of here before I descend on you" I refused to move.

"My God, where did I get this son from" Happy came back and heard mummy shouting.

"Mummy, mummy what's happening?"

"It's this stupid brother of yours, he insulted me" Happy became so furious.

"Tom you insulted mummy?"

"I didn't insult her" I replied

"So I am now a liar?" My mummy asked. I stared at her blankly and she removed her shoe and threw it at me.

"I said get out of here," she screamed.

"Tom didn't you hear her? She said you should get out of here," Happy said pushing me towards the door. I left angrily.

"Mummy, daddy is the one causing all these problems", Happy continued. "Honestly he's spoiling Tom…"

Those days our family was divided into two camps, as there was war in our house. My dad and I were in the same camp while mummy and Happy were in the other. It was like the girls against the boys. The quarrels continued until our new baby was born. A pretty baby girl was added to our family. She was actually a premature, born after seven months to be precise. I was very happy to have a little sister at last but my happiness was short lived as I left for secondary school just a week after she was born. She had to be incubated; because she was so tiny and weak… the Doctor said she might die. Early days in secondary school was like been in hell for me as I spent most of my time worrying about my little sister and was home sick all the time. This continued until my school father arrived… On my first visiting day, only my dad came as the rest of the family were at the hospital with our baby. Daddy had to rush back after assuring me that the baby was getting bigger and better with every passing day. The next visiting day is one that I would never forget in my life. The whole family came with my little sister, and she had grown so big! We held a little party right at the visiting ground. Mummy brought food and drinks in abundance and any student who cared to come ate to his or her fill. That day I held my little sister in my arms for the very first time, and then I realized sadly that I didn't know her name. When she was born, there was no time for naming but praying for her survival.

"Mummy what's her name?" I asked

"Ooh!" they all exclaimed

"How terrible, we forgot to tell Tom her name" my dad said.

"Her name is Yvonne". Happy informed me gladly.

"What a lovely name, I said lifting her high then I brought her face to face with me. Her eyes were so large and white.

"Hello Yvonne" I'm your big brother…"

Chapter 3

I WASN'T A SHY guy hence making friends was very easy for me but keeping those friends was a problem because I easily got bored and moved on to the next available person whom I could learn something new from. As I was neither an introvert nor an extrovert I suffered a lot of mood swings, today I would be an extrovert chanting everywhere and the next day I would be an introvert. Finding ones self in between two moods is something very disagreeable. I was called names like snub, scrub, feeler and many others. This made me a loner in primary school.

In secondary school, I adjusted by becoming a full-fledged extrovert and this attracted lots of friends to me like bees to honey. I made lots of friends but just one very good one, as there are friends and there are friends. A lot of people could never really understand what made us that close especially our parents. To be honest I myself cannot explain how we got that close.

My best friend's name was Mac or should I say is Mac because since after him I've met none like him. Mac was dad's friend Mr. Donald's son. Every Sunday my dad and I would go to their house. Our fathers were chess freaks as much as they were golf freaks. Saturdays were for golf at the club while Sundays were for chess at the Donald's residence.

While my dad played away I would always stand somewhere watching jealously as Mac and his younger brother Tony played football. "Why the hell don't I have a younger brother?" I'd wondered. Tony and Mac were both older than me. Believe me they were first class snubs and bullies, it was as if I didn't even exist, as they never noticed me. One day when I finally summoned courage and asked if I could join them in the game, they could not believe it. They laughed so loudly that it was as if my question evoked the god of thunder. "Look at this small rat" Tony said to Mac, "He is not even afraid"

"Come", said Mac bending down to level with me, I became frightened as Mac held me by my collar, it was as if he was going to strangle me.

"You said you want to do what?" he asked. I knew that my answer would determine if I was going to be strangled or not.

"I just wanted to watch" I replied

"That's better," said Mac arranging my collar properly. "You can watch"

I could not stand the humiliation so I ran away from the football pitch and searched for my friend and equal- their younger sister Kate who was suffering from sickle cell anemia. Mac was five years older while Tony was three years Older than I was.

When I was about going to school we went to their house, it was on a Sunday. Mr. Donald and his wife met us at the door.

"How is the baby?" They chorused

"Still in the incubator" my dad replied. "But she's doing fine"

"Thank God" they chorused again

"I thought you were not coming," said Mr. Donald

"You think I would miss playing Chess with you for anything?" My dad replied.

"He was already boasting that you developed cold feet," said Mrs. Donald.

"You don't say," replied my dad and they all laughed.

"Tommy how are you?" Mrs. Donald inquired.

"I'm fine ma"

"Big boy now," said Mr. Donald patting my head.

"You are going to start secondary school tomorrow right?"

"Yes sir" I replied.

"I have told Mac to be your school father, there are a lot of bullies in that school, you know. But never mind, mighty Mac will chase all the bullies". At first the news got me excited, Mac my school father? It was too good to be true. At last we were going to be close! But then I remembered the incidence at the football pitch and became apprehensive.

"Please darling, take Tommy to his school father, and bring us some hot tea" Mr. Donald said.

"Come on, speak for yourself" my dad cut in.

"What do you want?" Inquired Mr. Donald.

"Hot tea of course" he said, and they all laughed. He continued "don't tell me that you didn't keep those delicious akara and bread of yours for me".

"Of course" replied Mrs. Donald, "your usual is always here for you, look how he's salivating," she said pointing at my dad and they all laughed.

"Come on darling get it fast else we'll be swimming in his saliva soon". They all laughed again.

I left with Mrs. Donald feeling nauseated. Their sense of humor was so terrible, I could never smile at what made them throw themselves on the floor laughing because they had such a weird sense of humor, which I found disgusting. 'Swimming in a pool of saliva' wasn't funny to me at all, but so disgusting that Just imagining it made me want to throw up. Mrs. Donald was my mum's reverse; she was a full time housewife though she had a supermarket in town, she was hardly ever there. My dad loved and adored her and once told me that he wished mummy was like her. When we got to the parlor, the children were watching a movie. The guys did not notice me as usual but Kate rushed to meet me and we talked in low tones, believe me our voice was so low that someone two centimeters from us would not hear a sound but Mr. Mac yelled at us.

"Can't you people talk somewhere else" it shocked me and got me wondering, Mac sure does have a very sensitive antenna attached to his ear. We left the sitting room to the dinning area and continued our discussion.

"Are you still going to boarding school?" Kate inquired.

"Of course" I replied gladly, "I am leaving tomorrow, how about you?"

"They said I cannot go because of my sickle cell condition, they feel that I'll die there. Tom why are they so worried about me? I feel so afraid" then she started sobbing I didn't know what to do

"Look Kate" I said holding her face between my palms, "Kate, God has seen all your sufferings, I promise you, Kate that won't die of sickle cell anemia".

"Are you sure Tom?" She said getting excited

"Yes" I replied suddenly feeling like a small god; at least that consoled her and made her stop to crying.

"How about your sister, sorry I didn't ask you must think I'm wicked".

"No, No I don't think that you're wicked at all, I understand, she's fine but she's still in the incubator"

"I hope she gets better soon"

"I hope so too"

"Tom I don't like this house"

"Come on, your mum is always here for you"

"Always here for me? Tom she makes me sick, I can't blink my eyes without her asking what happened. If I sneeze she would start questioning me, its terrible with her, she makes me feel abnormal..."

I felt pity for her. I was the only one that knew what she was going through and I was very scared for her, because then I had the impression that, people with sickle cell anaemia could not live long. Later Kate's mum came with Akara and bread for Kate and I; then she sat down to chat with us.

"Tom I hope you have prepared for the task ahead?" She asked.

"I guess I have, but why won't you allow Kate go to a boarding school?"

"Tom you misunderstand, Kate is my only daughter, you cannot compare yourself with her you are a boy, boys are always stronger than girls, you know"

Mac went to get akara from the table and overheard his mum.

"Mummy what are you saying? Don't give him that crap you mean that Tom and I are stronger than you and Kate because you are girls?"

"Mac I am not a girl but a woman, and I was referring strictly to boys and girls" she replied.

"I still don't believe that boys are always stronger than girls," he said laughing at his mum.

"Look Tom, I am now your school father so prepare," he said to me then left.

"Anyway" continued Mrs. Donald, "Kate is a sickler, and we love her so much. Our major concern is what could happen when she has a crisis in school? Who would help her?"

"Are you afraid that she'll die?" I asked.

"Of course, crises without proper management could lead to death," replied Mrs. Donald.

"But if God says she'll die, she will no matter where she is".

"Hmmm" said Mrs. Donald, and who told you that?" she inquired.

"Pastor" I replied proudly, "he said that God's will always prevails"

She nodded in agreement, "you have a point there Tom, I guess nothing might convince you otherwise, you have a mind of your own and I like that, I wish I had a son like you..." Wow! That made me happy; knowing that someone appreciated me was an ego booster. Unlike my mum who always asks God where she got me from, Mac's mum wished she had a son like me.

"So Tom you'll be leaving tomorrow?" Kate inquired.

"Yes I replied but I'll call you always"

"Alright, I will also write to you always"

"Tom" my dad called out, "let's get out of here" The next day before I went to school I made a call to the Donald's but I could not speak to Kate as she was said to be in a critical condition. She had a crisis the previous night. I felt bad but I spoke with Mac instead.

"What do you want" Mac yelled and I became lost for words.

"Em actually..." I stammered. "I just wanted to find out when you'll be coming to school"

"Why do you want to know?" he inquired. "It's just em... that I don't want to be bullied by seniors if my school father..."

"Look Tom" he cut in. "you must be bullied, your tails must be cut off so just get prepared"

"But Mac, your dad said you'll take care of all the bullies"

"It's a pity, I am not going to be able to do much of that because I am not a final year student, but of course I'll be able to protect you from JS 2 to SS 1 students". That day I left for school feeling miserable. My dad took me alone as mummy was at the hospital with our baby. Immediately my dad's car was out of the gate I became sick. Sweat broke out from all over my body and my stomach started churning, next thing there was total blackout... Those early days in school I was always sick, but all my sickness disappeared when Mac arrived. School became fun for me.

I moved into Mac's room and was shocked at how nice he was. This was how our relationship started, from school father and son to best of friends. We were inseparable. Mac was a bully so most students were afraid of him. It was like I was hanging around with the toughest guy in school. Mac graduated in my JS3 and that was the first time I experienced heartbreak school became boring for me. It took me two terms to get used to not having Mac around. Courtesy of Mac, I became very popular in school amongst students and teachers. I had physical strength as I was one of the biggest guys in school and I was a big bully! Yes, I became a bully because in those days bullies were the most intelligent, well-respected and popular students.

I was also good in basketball just like Mac. The love and close-ness that erupted between Mac and I was unbelievable. We became so fond of each other; it was just like the love between David and Jonathan in the bible, except that ours was stronger. During the holidays we were inseparable because we were always together; this got my dad worked up.

As I strolled into the house one night my dad called me.

"Tom what time is it?" He asked. I looked at my wristwatch.

"Its 8.45 dad"

"Where are you coming from at this ungodly hour?"

"8.45pm is not ungodly" I replied

"Tom at your age it is ungodly, you are in SS 2 and you come home by 9pm, tell me what will happen when you get into the University?" I kept quiet.

"Now tell me where you are coming from"

"Mac's house" I replied. "I went for driving lessons"

"Mac's house" he said nodding.

"And where were you yesterday?"

"Mac and I went to the library to read"

"That is great" he replied sarcastically, "you guys went to read, what about two days ago, I can guess where you went to but I might be wrong, so tell me Tom where were you on Tuesday?"

"I was with Mac" I replied

"I knew it Tom, but can't you see that you're overdoing it? Don't you have other friends?"

"I don't dad".

"Then I suggest you make some friends that are in your class, so that you could discuss school work together".

"I discuss school work with my mates in school, at home I read as much as I can"

"But Tom, Mac is too old to be your close friend".

"Mac is my school father not my friend"

"School father? But Tom Mac has graduated what school father are you still talking about?" I had no answer to that.

Chapter 4

HAPPY BIRTHDAY TO you
Happy birthday to you
Happy birthday dear Thomas
Happy birthday to you
How old are you now
How old are you now
How old are you now
How old are you now
He's 17 years today
He's 17 years today
He's 17 years today
He's 17 years today
They all chorused
Many happy returns, many happy returns many happy returns
Happy birthday to you
Hip hip hip hurray!
Hip hip hip hurray!

"This birthday is not an ordinary celebration but it is also a thanks giving service in honor of my beloved son Tom, in whom I am well pleased..." everyone laughed.

"Tom is a great achiever. He passed WAEC brilliantly with seven distinctions. His JAMB result just arrived and he scored 320. "Wow" everyone chorused and they all gave me a standing ovation. "Come here" my daddy said holding out his hand "say something," he whispered into my ears.

"I thank everyone here for making it to my birthday. Mummy thanks very much for organizing such a wonderful party..." she smiled at me.

"Thanks to dad of course for providing the money, and thank God mostly for providing dad with the money" There was another standing ovation. "Thanks to my sister Happy for decorating the house with these beautiful balloons, I am very grateful Happy for your time considering your final exams which you are writing now. I thank Kate and Yvonne for the very beautiful birthday song, even though I would have preferred something new"

"oh oh" they all chorused.

"Yes" I continued. "I would have preferred something special composed by them for me because, every year for the past seventeen years I've heard the same birthday song". They all laughed. "How do I thank Mrs. Donald for the most beautiful cake I've ever set my eyes on?" Everyone hailed her. "And of course, I thank Mac, for all the moral support he gave me throughout my secondary school, I could go on and on but I guess you'll all sleep on me"

"Yes, Yes" they echoed

"Alright, I will live to remember each one of you; your presence has made my birthday special. Believe me, today is going to be an unforgettable day...Oh my God look at my presents!" I exclaimed and they give me another standing ovation.

At the end of the party every one left but Tony and Mac stayed back to help us clean the house. As we moved chairs inside I confided in Mac.

"My dad wants to change my course from engineering, he has even written an application."
"But you've always wanted to become an engineer" he replied, "you're so good in physics and mathematics what course does he want?"

"Business management then a higher degree in Accounts and Audit, he said he desires to hand everything over to me"

"Do you want to run his company?" Mac inquired

"I don't know" I replied. "As the only son it's like I have no choice"

"Thank God I'm not the only son" Mac replied. "I have my dreams Tom, if I work for my dad I won't excel in my career. Everyone will think you're getting promoted because you're the boss son. They just see you as a figure head, you understand?"

"I do. I do Mac, but I'm so confused"

"Talk to your dad about it, I see no reason why you should change your course if you really don't want to"

"I don't want to let him down Mac, I honestly don't want to"

"May be you should let yourself down instead," replied Mac. This really hit me. Let myself down? I dare not. I went to see my dad that night.

"I am so proud of you my son, where did you get that speech of yours?"

"What speech?"

"Come on Tom you had the crowd spellbound didn't you see how they were all clapping for you?"

"Believe me dad I can't even remember what I said"

"Then you are an orator my son"

"Daddy you are exaggerating"

"Seriously, all my friends commended you, from today you will write my speeches"

"I'm flattered dad"

"Did you enjoy the party?" he asked

"It was fantastic" I replied. "I wanted to talk to you about that change of course thing; I don't want you to send the application."

"Why my son? Professor Ajayi has started pursuing the issue"

"I don't want to read Business management"

"Why my son? Why?"

"I don't know what to say dad, it's just that I am very good in my science subjects".

"That's life for you" he said, "You have to learn how to make sacrifices for those you love. Tom, God loved us so much that he sent his only begotten Son that whosoever believes in him shall not perish but have everlasting life! Tom I want you to give everlasting life to my company"

"But I've never wanted to work at the company" I protested.

"Jesus Christ never wanted to suffer in this sinful world" he replied.

"Daddy, you are getting fanatical over a non-issue".

"You call an empire I built all my life a non-issue?"

"No dad, I didn't mean it that way"

"You are my first son Tom, my only son"

"Mac is his dad's first son but he's not going to run their company"

"Hear yourself talk, I knew it, I knew Mac had something to do with your decision"

"No dad, Mac has nothing to do with it"

"You worship Mac, Tom anything he says or does is the best, you want to be like him. This was not how I brought you up, I always listened to you, and never even tried to make you be like me and see what I get. You obviously want to become Mac's image. Tom I brought you up to chase the shadows of God. Each time I expect you to say, "all right dad I'll pray about it" I keep hearing Mac, Mac, and Mac. Please go away, I've had enough of you for one day". That was the first serious argument I had with my dad. It was also the first time he walked me out of his room. When I got to my room, Mac and Tony were already asleep. On that night of my seventeenth birthday I laid down to sleep engrossed in my thoughts. Was I really chasing Mac's shadow? If I was I would have read law just like him... I finally decided to read Business Administration, what was the point of disappointing my poor father who had worked very hard all his life building this empire just for me. My dad was right. I was overdoing it. I decided to apologize to him the next morning.

"Good morning son" he replied smiling at me, my heart melted the more I could not believe that he would smile at me.

"Daddy sorry about yesterday"

"Yesterday? What happed yesterday?"

"We had an argument".

"Oh that, I'm supposed to be the one apologizing for ending your birthday in that manner I guess I ruined your day".

"No dad, you didn't I chose that day to confront you it's my fault"

"Tom forget yesterday, you are going to be an engineer, a great one. I am ashamed I ever attempted to change your dreams"

"Daddy I had a rethink last night and decided to change my course"

"No Tom, you don't have to, and it's surprising that you never asked me why I didn't give you a birthday present"

"You didn't give me a present?"

"No I didn't"

"I've not opened most of the parcels anyway; I guess that's why I didn't notice. But daddy, on a serious note I've made up my mind, I want you to submit the application"

"Are you sure?"

"Yes dad, I've never been sure of anything like this in my life"

"I think you should still think about it, come and have your birthday present" He took me to the garage and behold a very beautiful car. A Mercedes Benz C-Class! I was dumbfounded as he handed me the keys. I didn't know what to say or do. I just stood there.

"I hope you like it"

"Like it?" I asked. "I love it dad, thank you very much"

I rushed upstairs and called Mac who also could not believe it. "Such a cute car" he said. Mummy, Yvonne and Happy also came to the garage.

"Get in Mac, Let's go for a ride," I said. My mum, dad, Happy and Yvonne watched me drive out of the house with my first car.

Happy was obviously jealous, she wasn't smiling at all like other members of our family. The car was black, smooth and sleek. After cruising for a while we stopped somewhere to admire the car. "Tom let's have a look at the engine" Mac said. I opened the bonnet.

"How was yesterday?" Mac inquired.

"I've never had a more beautiful birthday" I replied.

"That's not what I'm talking about Tom"

"What then are you talking about?"

"I was talking about your change of course, did you discuss it with your dad?"

"Oh! That, I busted it Mac, I'm going to study business management"

"My God Tom, don't give me the impression that this car changed your destiny"

"How dare you speak to me like that? I am tired of your meddling into my affairs okay, keep your stupid impressions to yourself because my destiny can never be changed" I yelled at Mac banged the bonnet and entered the car. Mac wanted to enter the car, but the door was locked so he knocked motioning me to open the door.

"Look Mac" I said after winding down the glass "stay out of my life forever". I drove off leaving him in the middle of nowhere without any money…I felt stupid afterwards. Mac obviously meant no harm but I could not just understand my outburst. Perhaps I was frustrated and wanted to vent my frustrations on someone or maybe I hated Mac subconsciously for making my dad and I drift apart. I felt wicked leaving him stranded, so I went back. Mac was already strolling down the road when I got to him.

"Mac, get in let's go home. I'm sorry…. I didn't mean what I said" Mac just stared at me.

"Please Mac, let's get out of here"

"Tom, I only asked because I care, I apologize for meddling into your affairs, I should have known that your silence meant you didn't want to talk about it. I swear never…"

"Stop it Mac, please stop it, I told you I'm sorry. I guess I was angry with myself. Please let's put this behind us and get out of here" Mac entered the car and we drove off. Before five minutes, we were chatting like nothing happened. He had put everything right behind him. We played basketball at their house, took our baths together and my dad was frantic as usual. During dinner daddy would not talk to me. I could not understand his anger because I called the house twice informing them about my activities. Happy was happy of course; Seeing daddy and I at loggerheads was one of the things that gave her joy. Yvonne broke the silence. "Tom tomorrow you'll take me with you to Mac's house in your new car right?"

"Of course" I replied.

"Tom, don't you get sick of going to Mac's house every day?" Happy inquired

"Of course I don't, do I look sick to you?" I replied sarcastically.

"Daddy" she continued, "things are going to get worse now that you've bought a car for him".

"Happy, it has nothing to do with the car" replied my mum "besides Mac comes here every day too, it's surprising that none of you have noticed"

"Alright" Happy said, "let's forget about the car, what does Tom do in this house? Tom, what do you do in this house?"

"What do you mean?" I asked

"What I mean Tom is that for example, I sweep the house every day, Yvonne washes the dishes and water the plants, you understand what I mean now right?"

"I guess I do but there's nothing for me to do Chioma does every other thing"

"Of course, Chioma could wash the dishes and sweep the house as well, but we help her out, you would be of great help by emptying the waste bin once in a while you know."

"Emptying the waste bin?" This girl is crazy I said to myself. But I didn't utter a word; silence was definitely the best answer I could give to Happy.

"Daddy", she continued, "Tom is spoilt silly and you worsened things up by giving him that flashy car for a birthday present at just seventeen"

"I bought it for his school, he won't be schooling here you know"

"How beautiful, but you never bought a car for me and I'm through with school now"

"Happy, your school is right in this town besides; the driver takes you to school and brings you back everyday"

"But daddy I am going for my house job in Port Harcourt, will the driver be taking me to the hospital there? I am the one, who needs a car dad not Tom. I wonder if I am really your daughter"

"Stop this" daddy yelled at her. "You are jealous of your own brother, your own flesh and blood".

"Why should I be jealous of him, I am just sorry for him that's all, you are ruining his life. He has no idea how difficult it is in the outside world and you won't help him find out...."

My dad could take no more, he stood up quietly and left. She was speaking the truth but there was nothing he could do about it because He loved me so much that he could not bear to see me suffer.

Immediately my dad left, I took my leave and headed straight for the phone to call Mac.

Chapter 5

FAMILY PROBLEMS WERE something that all my dads' money could not prevent. With everyone having his own personality and ideas little squabbles here and there are absolutely inevitable. It's funny but my little sister; Yvonne and I also had clashes. Is there is a saying that every family has skeletons in their closet… well, the first skeleton that was discovered in our family was found in Happy's closet. That calamity left me astounded for a long time… That day I was in Mac's house where we were preparing to go for a birthday party. It was actually Tony's new 'catches' birthday. Tony had never given us any moment rest since the day he met her. He said all manner of things about her that Mac and I were looking forward to meeting her. Tony organized the party for her to impress her. He wanted to give her a party that she would never forget in her life. The party was supposed to start by 7pm and I was trying on a shirt when my mum called.

"Your dad wants you home for dinner" she said

"But mummy I told you about the party I have to attend"

"I know but your daddy said your presence is of utmost importance"

"What time is the dinner?"

"8pm, Tom you have to come"

"I'll come anyway but I'll be thirty minutes late"

"No problem, just make sure that you come"

I felt terrible because my dad was about to ruin my day.

"What's up?" Mac asked

"They want me home for dinner"

"Oh oh!" he exclaimed

We got to the party arena early. Tony and his friends were busy getting everything in order.

"Hey Tom, Mac come here," said Tony

"Help me move that table, thanks guys" he said as we carried the table. Tony was over excited.

"Where is she?" I asked after thirty minutes, a lot of girls had arrived then.

"She'll be here soon," Tony replied.

When the party started everywhere was full with everyone doing his own thing chatting, dancing, drinking... you know what happens at parties but our honey didn't show up. Tony was already nervous. He was sweating like a chicken about to be slain. No, chickens don't sweat. He was sweating like a ram about to be slaughtered for Id El kabir; I don't think that rams sweat either... I'll have to find out about sweating animals I suppose. Anyways, he was sweating like an anxious person would. It was as if a bucket of water was emptied over his head. Mac was worried just like me and he tapped me.

"Tom it's like someone has been stood up"

"Exactly what I was thinking, it's already 7p.m and the celebrant isn't here" Mac called Tony to our side.

"Tony what's happening, where is she?"

"I don't know, I honestly don't know" he replied.

"Maybe we should go to her house and find out," I suggested.

"I don't think so," Tony replied. "I know she'll come just be patient and calm"

I could not believe it, whom was he telling to be calm? He was the one that was supposed to be patient and calm, he kept gulping alcohol and was almost drunk. I felt sorry for him… the next minute he jumped up.

"That's my girl" he winked at us rushing to the entrance to meet her. Mac and I rushed after him. Linda wasn't alone; she was with a hefty looking guy and wow, how cute she was.

"Hello" said the hefty looking guy. "I am Henry and who amongst you guys is the generous Tony?"

"I am" Tony answered taking Henry's hand in a handshake

"Oh" Henry said still shaking Tony "it's a pleasure finally meeting you, thank you very much for organizing my girlfriend's party. Believe me you can't imagine the amount of energy and cash you saved me."

Tony started laughing; it was unbelievable I myself could not understand

"Your girlfriend?" Tony asked. "Yes" he replied with a nod. Then Tony turned to Linda,

"Is he your boyfriend?"

"Yes" she replied. "He's my sweetheart. I told you I was seeing someone didn't I?"

"You sure did" Tony said dishing her a slap.

"How dare you" shouted Henry who jumped at Tony. They started fighting fiercely thereby disrupting the party. Everyone became confused, as there was utter chaos. Some guys finally took Henry outside, while some other guys and I tried to calm Tony down inside.

After a while Tony left saying that he wanted to get a drink. We allowed him since he wasn't going outside where Henry was. Before we knew what was happening, Tony had taken on Linda. He was punching hard at her and she was scratching him all over with her claws, sorry fingers. There was blood all over. We rushed there and tried to get Tony off her. It was difficult because Tony held on firmly to her braids and she was screaming. Damn women, all the other girls were screaming too. Those outside were having a hard time with Henry who wanted to come in. Finally, Tony let go of Linda pulling off some of her braids, and the girl fainted! Those that couldn't stand the sight of blood started vomiting. We finally bundled Tony into the car while Henry and some other people took Linda to the Hospital. For the first time I witnessed Mac and Tony quarrel. Mac was very angry and he slapped Tony so hard that Tony began to bleed from the mouth. I stood in the gap once again like an intercessor.

"Please Mac, don't start another fight," I pleaded.

"Another fight?" Mac inquired. "How can this coward fight me? What if he killed her, Tom what if she died?"

"It would have been better if she died" Tony said, "I wish I killed her. She thinks I am a fool, you would have allowed me kill the silly bitch".

"Hear him," Mac, said, "who is the silly person here? Tony you are the silly bastard, how could you beat a girl like that, you have definitely made a fool out of yourself".

"I agree Mac, but I don't feel like a fool, if I had not dealt with her I would have felt like one but how good l feel" Tony said smiling.

"Please, please and please you guys, let's get out of here, the police might come…" that made them snap into their senses. We jumped into the car. Tony's friend Brian came seriously hailing Tony obviously he was very pleased with him.

"Tony my guy, Tony you didn't let me down, I love the way you dealt with her I was actually about to take on her myself"

"Shut up" Mac yelled at him. "Tom let's go" I started the ignition but Brian ignored us and continued

"Tony don't worry, if they bring the police I'll know how to handle them, I'll pack the remaining drinks and other things then meet you at home, men I love you for what you did" he finished. I dropped Tony and Mac at their house. Tony went inside immediately but Mac was still furious.

"Mac its okay she didn't die at least"

"Tom, what if she died, what would I tell my parents, of course he'll go to prison. My only brother Tom, how will I survive without Tony?" I felt a stab of jealousy. I had no idea that Mac loved Tony that much because I thought I was the one he loved most.

"Tony is such a fool" he continued, "He thought he could buy the girl with money, not all girls are money freaks you know"

"Come to think of it Mac" I said. "Tony is somehow justified, Tony took so much pains to organize her birthday at least she would have had the decency of not bringing her boyfriend"

"I don't really blame her Tom, no girl is worth forcing into a relationship. She told Tony that she had a boyfriend but he still went ahead"

"Tony thought she was just playing hard to get"

"Look Tom, you need to see the chain of girls that are after me in school. I don't ask a girl out more than once, if she refuses, that's the end because pestering them makes them take you for granted"

"What a day! Let me rush home for dinner Mac, see you to-morrow" I got home before 8pm and my mum was surprised.

"Wow! Tom, what happened, you are home early"

"Mummy there was no party, it was a fight"

"Fight? Who fought?" she inquired.

"Tony and someone, the party was turned upside down."

"You see, that's why I don't buy this idea of partying around, it turns into violence more often than not" Yvonne walked in.

"Tom you refused to take me to your party but Kate took me to Uncle Ben's birthday"

"Who is Uncle Ben?" I inquired.

"Uncle Ben is Kate's doctor, they don't have any children, all their children died of sickle cell anemia…"

There was a knock at the door, my mum went to get the door and behold our lawyer. He asked to see my dad.

Yvonne was sent to get daddy, we thought that the lawyer wanted to deliver a message, but to our utmost surprise the lawyer ate dinner with us.

"Congratulations" the lawyer told Happy "when are you going for your House Job?"

"Next week" she replied

After dinner we went to the sitting room and sat down chatting. My dad told the lawyer to bring out some documents, which he asked Happy to sign. We could not understand. Happy was so excited, and was about to sign when my dad stopped her.

"For as long as you live, listen carefully and it applies to all of you, learn to go through any document very carefully before signing. It's even preferable to have your own lawyer also go through them before you ever commit yourself, all right?"

"Yes dad." We all replied. "Thanks for the advice" Happy said smiling and she started going through the papers. Suddenly her countenance changed and she became very angry.

"What's wrong? Happy, what's happening, what's happening?" my mum demanded looking at my dad.

"Young lady, would you sign right away or you would give them to your lawyer for proper advice?"

"Yes" Happy said. "My lawyer will get back to you". The lawyer bade us good night and left. Immediately he shut the door behind him, Happy tore the papers into shreds.

"Nonsense" she said. I am not signing anything, I don't have to be your daughter, I disown you dad, there's no need drawing up those legal documents"

"Someone tell me what's happening" my mum demanded

"Your daughter is a prostitute and a disgrace to my personality. She has even had an abortion"

"What abortion?" Asked my mum.

"Happy, is it true?"

"Yes mum, it's true, I did it just once, and I did it because I realized that the man was married…he lied to me and promised we would be together till eternity…"

My mum started crying.

"I provide everything for you but you pay me back by tarnishing me image and making me a laughing stock of this community, I disown you, pack your things and leave my house. I can't live with you else the devil will tempt me into killing you with my bare hands" my dad retorted.

"Oh Happy, why didn't you come to me", why didn't you tell me. What if you had lost your life, oh Happy…" said my mum in tears.

Happy started sobbing and Yvonne joined her. I could not just utter a word or move.

"Look" my mother said wiping away a big tear, "you cannot disown her for this, you have no right it was a mistake, a lot of girls terminate pregnancies every day. I work in the hospital and know how men lure young ladies into shameful acts"

"My daughter is not a lot of girls okay, I didn't bring her up to become a murderer, I gave her the best of everything, the best education, a very high standard of living…and everything, yet she was sleeping around with some old married man"

"Happy, why didn't you ever introduce any of your male friends's to us?" My mum inquired.

"Oh mummy" Happy answered still sobbing, "there was never time, you were always at the hospital and I've never been close to daddy".

"Happy you would have confided in me anyhow, we would have made out something" Mummy replied. Happy was still crying.

"I'll give you some money tomorrow, when I come back to the house I don't want to see you, but you can take the Honda or the Mercedes."

"Daddy you can't be serious" I said, "please hear her out."

My dad went straight to his room and I went after him.

"Daddy she is sorry, she has explained everyth…"

"Being sorry does not wipe away a sin Tom, she has to be disciplined, and she has to be punished".

"Yes dad, I agree but this punishment is too severe"

"Too severe? Are you saying the punishment is not appropriate? God, she has sinned against her body and the baby she killed, that child would have made an impact in our lives. Tom every child is created by God to serve a purpose, that child was to come and serve a purpose"

"Daddy I know all these, let's allow God and her conscience judge her. God's punishment is going to be worse than this one"

"No Tom, I am not punishing her. I am merely disciplining her; remember what God did to Eli because of his children? If it was you or Yvonne I would have done exactly the same" That statement got me tongue-tied. That was my dad anyway, a man of extremes. He always went to the extreme to do anything. When he loved, he loved to the extreme, just the way he loved me and when he hates, he does so to the extreme. His moral and religious standards were too high. I was very angry with him. I mean no one can ever be perfect. If my dad was God then everyone on the face of the earth would have been wiped out. Haven't all sinned and fallen short of the glory of God? It was a terrible day. First Tony nearly committed murder then the discovery that Happy had ended the life of an innocent child... I kept praying to God to make my dad change his mind and all of us kept pleading but he refused to reconsider. Happy left the house for her intership but she refused to take the car and the money. Our hearts were broken and shattered into tiny bits especially my mum. Daddy didn't show any emotion and mummy kept quarreling with him. She called him names like cold bastard, Mr. Holy and Mr. Perfect... Mac was there to comfort me. Two years later mummy told us that Happy was going abroad for further studies. Mummy, Yvonne and I traveled see her just to say goodbye. She told us all not to cry nor miss her, as she was coming back soon, but soon became a very long time.

Chapter 6

BEING IN A university was a memorable experience. Mac and I were schooling and living together once more. We were sharing an apartment; it was four of us actually Tony, Mac, Brian and I.

Brian was Tony's best friend; the two of them were womanizers and they were also seriously involved in women battering. Mac and I were the opposite, it's not that we hated girls, they were not just our priorities, the truth is that they were always chasing after us and that really got us irritated. Honestly Mac and I were the most sought after guys on campus because, we were rich, handsome, and intelligent. In a nutshell we had all it took to make girls go crazy about men.

Our best game remained basketball. I don't know how, but somehow we became alcoholics' not chronic ones anyway. Perhaps it was due to too much partying, you know at parties its either you chase the girls or you chase the bottles. The first girl Mac went out with was Tonia, they split up due to gross incompatibility and Rose was next. Rose was too demanding, what she wanted was Mac's money so he broke up with her too. After Rose was Buky. Buky wanted to run Mac's life. She was too domineering and Mac would have none of it. He called it quits.

Finally Angela came into our lives; she was a phantom of delight. Her voice was angelic, she could sing and dance, was a very good cook and most of all she looked ravishing as she had all the right curves in the right places. I was in love with Angela just like Mac who was also crazy about her but Angela was Mac's girlfriend. The feelings I had made me ashamed of myself but there was nothing I could do about it. I tried going out with other girls to forget Angela but it was not possible.

Usually when Mac's girl come to the house to visit, I would hang around for like fifteen minutes then disappear. But with Angela it was different. I would hang around for up to forty five minutes until Mac tells me bluntly to excuse them.

Angela became my very close friend because the three of us were together everywhere. I don't know how but somehow the love I had for Angela took another dimension perhaps I finally accepted her as Mac's girl.

When Mac graduated, it was as if I was dreaming, but I wasn't as shattered as I was when he left in secondary school. On the night of his last paper Angela, Mac and I went out to celebrate. We gulped so much alcohol that Angela got really furious and left angrily. We were already too far-gone to care about her as she stormed out. We drank so heavily that the hang over lasted for about three days. When Mac left for law school, he promised to come down to Ibadan after a month but he never showed up. Angela and I tried all avenues of reaching him but failed. Angela became angry the following week. When Mac had still not called, after two months she became hurt. Six months later, Angela became hysterical. I was there of course to comfort and reassure her that Mac still loved her. I was mad at Mac because I could not understand the reason he refused to get in touch with us. I kept calling his house but was told he's in law school and not at home.

One evening, Tony, Brain and I were watching a movie when the phone rang, Brain picked it up.

"Hey Mac" he yelled, "What's up with you?" I rushed there and grabbed the phone from him.

"What's wrong with you?" I shouted. "Why didn't you call?"

"Tom, I'm sorry, I've been very busy," he went on telling me how Law school was. "Tom, I've got to distinguish myself else I won't be called to bar" I was surprised that he didn't even ask after Angela.

"Are you not forgetting someone?"

"Who?" He asked. I was mad, "Angela of course"

"oh oh, Angela, how's she?"

"Terrible" I answered. "Its not fair how you neglected her, at least you would have sent her cards or something to say you care, she's always here crying and I'm beginning to get sick of covering up for you"

"Tom, you don't have to cover up anything I never promised Angela that I was going to marry her did I?"

"Are you asking me? How am I supposed to know what you promised and what you did not promise? Man, you are a cold blooded bastard"

"Hey Tom, come on, why are you so angry?"

"Any reason why I shouldn't be? You want to dump like this her after all you shared with her...without even a word?"

"Look Tom, it's over between us, it finished that night she walked out on us at oluyis? Remember how she poured her drink on my face?"

"She did that out of love Mac, she didn't want us to drink too much".

"Hmm you are now a righteous man Tom, that's very interesting but please stop encouraging her, it's over okay. I'm going out with someone else right now. Tom, if you see her you're going to shake she is..."

"Mac" I cut in, "I am not interested in hearing about who you are dating right now and I cannot tell Angela it's over okay? I won't, come and do it yourself"

"Na wa o, Tom you are really surprising me. Mr. righteous. Remember Carla? Who told her it was over? Was I not the one?

And Tom it was heartless the way you treated her, avoiding her, hiding inside the toilet, under the bed and inside the wardrobe… Who kept covering up for you?" I was just silent. "Tom are you there?" "Yes" I replied.

"Tom we'll make a deal, I'll make up with Angela on one condition"

"What condition?" I asked.

"I can only make up with Angela if you make up with Carla, No girl can ever be as good for you as Carla"

"Is that the only condition?"

"Yes Tom, it's so easy isn't it?"

"Yes Mac, it's the easiest thing in the world to do but fuck you Mac, fuck you!" Tony took the phone from me. I went straight to my room. It was terrible, Mac wanted to blackmail me! He knew that I could never go back to… God! She almost killed me…

Carla's story is so terrible that I still get embarrassed thinking about it; God, what ever brought her into my life…When Angela came that evening I had to tell her the truth. I knew she was going to cry but she had to know the truth as It was obvious that Mac had found someone else. It was a very difficult thing for me to do but I did it. She started laughing when I broke the news.

"Why are you laughing?" I inquired, "Tom, what do you expect? You want me to cry? Alright, to please you I am going to cry" then she started crying, she was actually wailing. I knew that Tony and his friend Brian were going to send her out of the house if they met her in that condition. The noise was loud so I did what I felt was right. I took Angela to my room and locked the door then I pleaded with her not to cry anymore to no avail. I had to provide a shoulder for her to cry on of course, and I stroked her hair and face, then we started kissing and before I knew what was happening we had gone all the way! It was a very spontaneous love making that ended within a few minutes.

I felt happy at first then guilty afterwards. Angela dressed up quietly and left without a word. I was really drained confused and so tired that I could not stand up to gather my clothes which were scattered all over the floor. Tony and Brian came home and I didn't even hear them come in. They came straight into my room.

"Tom, Thomas Tommy" Tony said. "I can see that you've been busy"

"No" Brian said, he has been very very busy, we are impressed Tom, more condoms in your wardrobe I'll advice" Tony and Brian laughed hysterically then left. "Wow" said Tony as they walked out.

"I wonder how many rounds he went to leave him so drained"

"I can guess" Brian said. Funny enough, I didn't feel embarrassed at all. I can imagine how ecstatic they would get if they knew who I just had it with because sleeping with the same girl was their favorite exploits. I felt dirty and hated girls. Angela's case was a mistake anyway neither of us planned it, but at least she should have stopped me. What would Mac say? Would he laugh it off and ask for more details just like Tony and Brian or would he feel sad? I decided it was going to remain a secret in fact I convinced myself that it never happened between Angela and I.

Three days later to my greatest surprise, Angela came with a bottle of wine, she said she wanted us to celebrate our love, I didn't know what to say because I had no idea what love she was talking about I guess she meant lovemaking... Then she was all over me, how weak my flesh was, we made love again and from that day it became a normal routine. We never talked about Mac, we gave the relationship our best shots and enjoyed ourselves but one day we said goodbye to each other in the best way we could, and no one was hurt because Angela became born again. I was somehow relieved because I was already tired of her, to say the truth I was fed up as our relationship was purely physical and I got too much too soon. I had to get close to Tony and Brain because we were in the same department but they were a year ahead of me. Business administration was not really a difficult course so we had time to party. Within two semesters, I had gone out with five girls! It was then that I realized that bad company could corrupt a good man. Tony and Brain graduated in my final year so I had a year to spend all by myself. At first I enjoyed the peace and quiet but later became miserable and lonely. It was that year I met Edith. Edith was a very outspoken girl in mass communication but she gave me a venereal disease the very once I had sex with her. Going to the hospital to be treated was very embarrassing for me. I could not just summon the courage, as it was a horrible sight I had down there and it became more horrible with every passing day. The pain was unbearable and worst when I was urinating. I decided to reduce water intake so as to prevent frequent micturation. It helped but I became so dehydrated and weak. Finally I summoned courage and went to the doctor, who was very angry that I didn't come for treatment on time; he informed me that I might have become sterile had I come a few hours later! He also said that the scars were permanent! The fucking scars from the sores were going to remain with me forever! He asked me to bring all those that I had sex with for treatment. I wanted to tell him that I wasn't a dog but just kept quiet. I thought of Edith, there was no doubt that she gave it to me. The bitch nearly ruined my life. The big question I kept asking myself was what to do with her. After thinking deeply I decided on a master plan…

That evening, I went to her department and invited her to my house she said I had to pick her up, as she was finishing her lectures by 6pm.

I drove into her department at exactly 6pm. She came with some of her friends and introduced us, I kindly said hello to them. Edith wanted me to give them a lift to town but I refused bluntly.

"I'm sorry I can't," I said. "Look at the one in the middle what's your name?"

"Sheyi" she replied smiling

"That's a lovely name I continued "but Sheyi is too fat I'm sure I won't be able to move the car if she enters and the other two are too tall, I won't be able to see my back, so sorry girls." I entered the car and Edith jumped in with me. The silly girl was very happy.

"Tom darling, I love the way you told them off"

"Really?" I was actually surprised,

"Yes Tom, they have been jealous of me ever since we started dating. They gossip about me, Sheyi the fat one said that you were just going to use me and dump me. Then Remi, the one in mini skirts said that she was going to snatch you from me because you are too much for me".

"Am I not too much for you?"

"How can you be too much for me?" she laughed. How stupid girls could be, I had already made up my mind about what I was going to do... Immediately we entered the house she rushed to the kitchen and brought a bottle of wine.

"Tom lets make a toast"

"Go back to the fridge and keep that wine," I said, "it's for someone"

"Who?" She demanded. "I'm sure it's a girl?"

"How did you guess, its for my sweetheart, she will be coming later" she didn't know what to say so she started laughing.

"Tom you are very funny"

"Shut up!" I shouted at her. "Don't ever call me funny okay, I am not a clown, have I made myself clear?"

"I'm sorry Tom, I see you're in a bad mood, I'll take my leave now"

"You are going nowhere Edith"

"Then better start behaving yourself if you don't want me to go..." before she could finish I gave her a slap

"Who are you to talk to me like that?" I asked. She could not believe it, she rushed to the door to make an exit but the door was locked. I went and grabbed her by the arm and gave her another slap. She ran to the dinning room, and started crying.

"Tom what's come over you? You are hurting me"

"By the time I'm through with you, you'll be more hurt" I replied.

"Please Tom, please let me go"

"Take off your clothes" I said and I started removing my belt

"Tom please, don't rape me, it's not fair, oh what have I done to deserve this," she cried and I laughed.

"Rape you? What makes you think that I want to rape you? You'll soon realize that there are other reasons why people take off their clothes... Hurry up" when she was completely naked I pounced on her like a wild beast and flogged her mercilessly. She kept shouting for help but the radio was loud so no one could hear her screams. I threw my belt away and took her with my bare hands. I punched her everywhere. She was bleeding from her nose and mouth and kept begging me for pardon. I became startled when I heard a key trying to open the door from outside, the next minute the door was flung open. Low and behold Mac.

"Tom, what's wrong with you?" I quickly shut the door and ushered Mac inside. "My God" he said when he saw Edith "now dress up and get out of here" I said to her. She tried to stand up but she fell. I brought out the letter I had written and threw it at her.

"Tom have you gone crazy?" Mac demanded, he quickly got some water and started cleaning her up. I went to the fridge got a cold bottle of gulder and started drinking.

"Tom two of her teeth are off" Mac cried out

"Mac please stay out of this" I replied "you won't even go near her if you know what she is." Mac took Edith and they left to God knows where. I was on my fifth bottle when he came back still furious.

"Where are you coming from?" I asked "From the hospital, I took her for treatment then took her to the hostel. I begged her not to tell anyone and I lied to her roommates that some thugs attacked her, I also gave her some money. I read the letter but how could you ever beat up a woman like that, she claims she does not have any venereal disease"

"It takes a longer period of time to manifest in women" I replied.

"What if you killed her Tom?"

"She infected me with herpes and syphilis, she's a whore and I don't care if she lives or die". Mac was lost for words

"She was like a saint Mac, I just discovered that she's an all-rounder that sleeps with anything that offers money"

"Hope you are better now?" Mac inquired

"Yes I'm getting better, the sores are still there, but they are dry-ing up, and I no longer feel pain when urinating"

"I'm sorry Tom, but thank God it's not HIV!" Mac gave me a heart touching sermon. That night I cried and felt so rotten, what if it was HIV? What would have become of me? Mac and I talked at length. I confessed to him about Angela and to my surprise he said that Tony told him everything. It was a shock because I was very discreet and had not the slightest impression that Tony knew! I was happy that I confessed anyway.

Mac told me how his girlfriend, the one he met at law school broke his heart and got married to a very influential military man. He became so depressed that no one could comfort him. He became Mac again when he found Jesus. Mac became born again. He told me about his sweet experiences with God and encouraged me to love God. That night we prayed together for the first time in our lives. I gave up girls but I could not give up drinking… Mac stayed with me for two weeks then, left for further studies in Canada. For the rest of my studies, I became a holy and righteous man and started going to church twice a week. Realizing how I had wasted my life caused me pain. I already had an extra semester from a 300 level course so I wasn't graduating with my mates, this also made me depressed. My extra semes-ter was a different experience, I had no friends except church members and took my studies and spiritual life very seriously… one afternoon, I went to the restaurant to eat and there sat the most beautiful sight I had ever seen in my life. I kept looking at her and fell in love with her at first sight but I could do nothing about it because I had given up girls.

After my lunch, I resisted the urge to go to her and fled. Days later I could not just forget the face I saw at the restaurant. I wished I had gone to express myself to her; finally I made up my mind that next time she comes my way I'd know just what to say…However, I was shocked to my marrow when a week later, when I saw her and a friend of hers' at my doorsteps! it was like a dream. God had finally answered my prayers.

"C..an I help y..ou?" I stammered.

"Are you Thomas Davis?"

"Yes" I replied.

"Thank God" they both chorused. I ushered them in and they told me their plight. They couldn't get accommodation and needed a place to stay so Tony's friend gave them my address. They begged to stay in my apartment until they got a place of their own. I had no choice but to accept them, after all I was staying in a four bedroom apartment all alone. That was how Tessy and Maria came into my life. They were so grateful when I told them that they could move in and I concluded that God really wanted Tessy and I to be together, how else could I explain the situation. I fell on my knees and begged God to strengthen me to overcome any temptation, which they may pose in my life.

The two of them were not bad girls. I became a big brother to them. Christ in me was radiating as my lifestyle spoke for me. The day I invited them to church they gave no excuse. That was the day they both gave their lives to Christ. The three of us became a family. We would go to school together, go to church together and other places. We took turns in cooking and sincerely speaking, I was the best cook. I guess I acquired my cooking skills from my stay with Mac, Tony and Brian. Being the youngest I had to do the cooking most of the time, as they were all lazy bones. Maria was the worst cook. We lived happily till I graduated.

Chapter 7

I STARTED WORK IN the company after my doctorate degree, which I got from London and moved back home. It was great being at home again with my parents and little sister Yvonne, who was at the school of nursing and midwifery, taking my mum's footsteps. We finally heard from Happy after nine years!!! She called to inform us that she was staying in Abuja with her family. Mummy even spoke with her husband on the phone. We were so excited that we took the next available flight to Abuja. Daddy refused to come with us and even ordered us not to go but this time we broke his commandment. Happy, her husband and three sons were all at the airport to receive us! There was no sleep that night because we had so much to talk about…. After two days with the family we decided to go back home but mummy would not hear of it, so Yvonne and I had to go back without her. We took photographs for daddy who also very surprised to know that he is a grandfather. He called my mum and asked her to come with the children, as he still didn't want anything to do with Happy but Happy refused to allow her children meet him…

I was made assistant manager after three months in the company, but in actual sense I was the managing director because my
dad left everything in my care. Mac was working for a small firm;
Tony was the managing director of his dad's company while Brian
was working for an oil company somewhere in Port Harcourt.
Mac and I were still close, in fact closer. Since after Angela, I felt
this stronger bond with Mac. Was it that men got closer after
sleeping with the same girl?

I didn't like where Mac was working, I wanted him to come
and work with me but I knew that he was not going to accept. A
perfect opportunity came one day; it was not really an opportunity
anyway because I orchestrated Mac losing his job. It was so easy.
All I had to do was to give the man in charge a handsome bribe,
asked him to dismiss Mac and he did just that. I sat in my office
so nervous as I knew that Mac was going to come straight to me.

"Hope I didn't get you out of something important?" Mac said
shutting the door behind him.

"Of course you did", I replied "but I don't mind"

"I was fired"

"What!"

"I said I was fired, sacked, chased out…"

"But they can't do that to you after all the time and energy you
put into that…damn" then I started weeping.

"Tom", Mac said surprised. "I can't believe this, you are over-
reacting and you know it, I feel you are pretending"

"What are you insinuating?" I inquired

"I'm insinuating nothing, come on you know I'm a lawyer, we
lawyers have a logical way of reasoning. We take tears to mean
guilt but I know you can't be responsible, it's just not possible. I'll
start looking for another job right away. I've got the qualification
haven't I? It's just annoying Tom, I was making a name in that
place I was making waves…"

"Oh Mac, what are we going to do? How about just going to
work for your dad?"

"No Tom, don't get on my nerves you know I'd rather remain
jobless."

As planned my secretary came in

"Sir it's time for the send forth

"What send forth?" I asked

"The send forth for barrister Irabor" she replied

"Oh I forgot I'd be there right away"

"Irabor is leaving?" Mac asked

"I thought it was a big joke when daddy said something like that, he is an old man anyway, he deserves rest... You see, God has just opened a way for you. You've gotten yourself a job"

"Really?" said Mac

"Of course" I replied, "if you want it, you've got it".

"But what about the board of directors?"

"I didn't say I was going to employ you, the board of directors will do that after they interview you. You're qualified and good, I'm sure you will pass the interview".

"I will write an application. Tom you can't imagine how relieved I am"

"Me too I said, look Mac I've got to rush I'll see you after work and please don't hit the bottles okay".

I left for the send forth and prayed to God to forgive me but I was very pleased with myself.

Mac got the job, so once again we were completely together. After work we would go out, play chess and finally go to our various houses. On Saturdays we would play basketball then go out somewhere and get drunk. Mac and I were both happy men but Mac's mum started pestering us about getting married; she nicknamed us 'old young men'. Mac really wanted to get married but there was no wife! Looking for a wife is not as easy as looking for a girlfriend you'll agree with me. Tessy and Maria completed their youth service two months before and were seriously job hunting. I prayed that Mac would fall in love with Maria so I invited them over they replied that they were coming after a month. A month was too far off l thought. How wrong I was, time flew so fast that I didn't know how one month passed, as I was bedridden for a month.

Chapter 8

I AM NOT A superhuman with supernatural health; once in a while I would have dysentery, flu, fever and mostly headache. The first serious illness I had was syphilis and herpes far back in the University, which left terrible scars all over my manhood. Believe me since then, going after women was something I could not do, no matter how interested I was, somehow the feeling just ended.

The second serious sickness I had nearly took my life. Firstly, I was diagnosed as having pneumonia and was placed on antibiotics… Mac was a kind of friend that was hard to find, so caring, loving and reliable. I can't explain it but he was just indispensable. I kept asking myself if I could ever live without him because he stood by me throughout. The sacrifices he made for me were beyond comprehension. My greatest problem was alcohol and I knew I could give it up if Mac asked me to, but Mac was also an alcoholic!

It was as if I would never get up from my sick bed, pneumonia left and something else that could not be diagnosed took over.

I became so thin. My blood was screened for HIV. Sincerely I thought I had it and was so relieved when the result came out negative. Every sickness they say originates from the mind that's why depressed, malnourished unhappy people are prone to diseases, but I wasn't in that category. I can't still explain what kept me on my sick bed. I mean I had everything; I had parents that loved me, had a good job, drove the best cars, wore the best clothes, and ate at first class restaurants yet I was sick. My sickness made me see my parents differently, somehow I discovered that my mum loved me very much, much more than I ever imagined. She brought traditional medicine when I was not responding to orthodox treatment. She told me that the herbalist informed her that some ancient demons in our village were after me; they wanted her only son dead. It was then that she discovered that my illness was not ordinary but spiritual.

She brought out a new razor blade and a kind of powder, which was wrapped in a paper; she cut me in strategic places and applied the powder. First was on my head probably to protect my brain, then my chest probably to protect my heart, my forehead followed probably to make me invincible and finally my hands that which I still can't explain.

The next day she brought a coconut, which she made me eat, I had to eat everything and drink all the water. She explained that I had secured my future.

"Tom no one can ever take your destiny away from you. You have your life right in your hands" she said.

On the third day she brought soap and asked me to bath with it. My mum did a lot of things. It was as if I was hypnotized, as I didn't question her. I just did as she said. Every evening, my dad, mum and some elders in our church would come and pray over me. At nights my dad would come alone and pray fervently for me, sometimes he would weep. Later he started plans of flying me abroad for proper checkup and treatment.

But to everyone's surprise and joy I got better at once. I just woke up that morning and realized I could stand up, I walked down stairs, sat at the dining and ate breakfast; I ate like a lion, as I was so hungry. It was celebration time again in the house. I kept wondering what helped me up, was it my dad's prayers, my mum's juju or the drugs? I finally concluded that the three were responsible. All things work together for good for those who love God. I thanked God for the kind of parents he gave me. Words cannot explain how grateful I was. A special thanksgiving service was held for my recovery. It was surprising that I never told Mac or my dad all my mum did, I didn't even have the urge to so it remained a secret between my Mum and I, just the two of us. A day after the thanksgiving service Mac was with me.

"Tom you've forgotten that Tessy's coming tonight right?"

"No" I said. "They are coming on the twelfth"

"Today's the twelfth" he replied "Here's a calendar Tom, have a look"

"My God, Mac what are we going to do?"

"I guess we'll take them out"

"No Mac, we won't take them out, I don't feel strong enough, get something lets have dinner here"

"Alright Tom, if you say..."

Yvonne ran into my room and startled us. I got so angry that I snapped at her.

"Don't you have simple courtesy? How many times do I have to tell you to knock before entering my room?"

"Come on Tom you..."

"Mac, stay out of this, what if one of us was naked?"

Yvonne became embarrassed.

"I'm sorry Tom, I heard you've been very ill so I rushed down just to see you, I can see you're okay now. Please pardon me" She banged the door behind her. I called out to her but she refused to come back.

"I strongly suggest that you see a psychotherapist Tom, you are screwed you know, all over"

"Mac please help me apologize to her"

"I can't Tom, I'm staying out of it see ya"

I peeped out and saw Mac walking towards her room and smiled knowing I could count on Mac to talk sense into her.

Something pushed me to eaves drop so after Mac shut the door behind him, I tiptoed to the door and watched from the keyhole.

"Stop punishing that food Yvonne, you don't have to eat if you don't want to," said Mac.

"Oh Mac, I thought he was really sick"

"Of course Yvonne, he was really sick but thank God he's better now"

"How dare he question my morals? He always vents his irritation on me, I traveled a long distance to see him only to come and be embarrassed and humiliated" then she started sobbing.

"Come here Yvonne, come on stop crying" she went to Mac and he cuddled her, "please stop crying he hasn't been himself lately and honestly you scared us" Mac continued stroking her hair and cleaning her tears, it brought back memories of Angela, this was how it all started… I almost opened the door but something held me back. Then Mac held her cheeks between his palms they were looking into each other's eyes.

"Yvonne, I'm going to town to get some things, maybe I'll just take you out somewhere and buy you a beautiful present for being such a good sister"

"No Mac, I don't feel like going anywhere"

Mac's hands fell to his side; I became relieved because the way he was holding her looked like he was going to start kissing her.

"I command you to get out of that uniform and dress up," he said sternly. "You are coming with me and I'm giving you just five minutes to get dressed okay"

"All right" she replied

Then he kissed her. It wasn't the kind of kiss I gave Angela anyway he kissed her on the forehead, Just the way he would kiss his sister. I ran back to my room. It was so kind of Mac. But I felt somehow, Mac kissing my sister's forehead wasn't really proper…

Mac entered my room.

"What's up Mac, you're back already?"

"Back from where?"

"From the supermarket of course"

"Oh, I've not even gone out of this house"

"How is she I asked?"

"Who?" Replied Mac

"Yvonne of course, were you not with her?"

"Whenever you hurt someone you find it difficult apologizing, you always want someone else to do it for you, anyway, we were not talking about you, we were talking about us, Yvonne and I"

I laughed, "Mac you are a bad liar, I know you talked sense into her"

"If you feel that way go to her room let's see what will happen to you"

"Please Mac get real"

"All right, I sure did talk to her but you've got to apologize too"

I went to Yvonne's room and knocked at the door

"Who is it?" she asked,

"It's your big brother"

"One minute please, I'm dressing up"

"You see, Yvonne think of how it would have been if I jumped into your room the way you did".

"This is different" she replied, "I'm not ill"

"Alright Yvonne, I'm sorry thanks very much for coming to see me, am I forgiven?" she opened the door

"Of course, Tom, it's just embarrassing that you shouted at me in front of Mac, at least you would have waited for him to leave before chastising me"

"Come on, you don't have to be embarrassed because of him he's just like your big brother…" Mac knocked and entered

"Yvonne lets get moving"

"Get moving where?" I asked as if I didn't know

"We are going out, what business of yours is it" Mac replied

"Yvonne where is he taking you?"

"I have no idea, but I'll go to the hospital to see mummy afterwards"

Chioma helped us prepare dinner for our guests while Mac and I waited for their arrival.

"Mac how do I look"

"Silly" he replied

"Oh Mac please tell me the truth"

"Alright Tom, you look like Adolph Hitler, mean and wicked!"

When the doorbell rang, we both disappeared from the sitting room because we didn't want them to catch us waiting for them. We were actually peeping from our hiding place but to our disappointment it was the lawyer.

"Good evening sir" Chioma greeted him

"Good evening pretty" he replied smiling mischievously

"I beg your pardon sir?"

"I said good evening pretty"

"Why Sir"

"What's wrong with it are you not pretty"

"Sir you don't have to flatter me"

"Chioma, I'm not flattering you, you are very beautiful and I've been admiring you for sometime now".

"Oga is not here and madam is at the hospital, what do you want"

"Chioma its you that I want, I love you…" I could not take it anymore. I was so disappointed in Mr Alexander. I could not just imagine the old man toasting our housemaid.

"Hello Mr. Alexander" I said, "hope I didn't interrupt anything" He was embarrassed

"No, I m..ean yes" he stammered,

"You came at the right time"

"Right time?" I asked

"Yes, I mean you know"

"What Mr. Alexander?"

"I came in yesterday and decided to check on the family"

"We are doing fine Mr. Alexander"

"I'll take my leave now, tell daddy I came okay". Mac and I could not help laughing when he left. It was so funny that Mr. Alexander professed love to Chioma!

"Mac I have to go and shave this moustache

"Come on Tom, I was only joking"

"I feel like Hitler already"

Finally Tessy and Maria did come. We ran into each other's arms.

"Hope you've forgiven me for not attending your graduation?" I asked

"Do we have any other choice?" Maria replied

"Tom I'm so happy you are back on your feet" Tessy said

"I am very grateful" I replied.

"You girls won't believe who's here"

"Who is it?" asked Maria.

"Someone you girls have been dying to meet"

"Mac" shouted Tessy.

"You guessed right, let me get him" I came back with Mac.

"This is Mac, and Mac, Tessy and Maria"

"I can't believe what I'm seeing," said Tessy

"Mac you are so cute"

"That's what a lot of girls tell me" he replied smiling

"Don't mind him," I said. "You're the first person to tell him that".

"Come on" said Maria. "He's cute", "Mac you are not photogenic at all, your picture doesn't look like you"

"Thanks for the compliment, both of you look exactly the way you looked in your pictures, very pretty girls. Let's get to know each other, are you girls still job hunting?"

"I have a job now said Maria, but Tessy is still jobless".

"Tell us about yourself Mac, what kind of Mac are you?" asked Tessy,

"I beg your pardon?" Mac replied

"I mean Tom calls you Mac, are you Mac or Mark"

"Oh, I'm macilinus, in primary school everyone called me Macleans, when I got to secondary school I didn't want anyone making fun of me so I settled for Mac".

"Students have a way of making life unbearable, in my primary school days I was called broom stick, shapeless, figure one and many other terrible names, because I was very thin" said Maria. "But look at me now".

We all laughed. We ate dinner and talked at length. I promised Tessy that I was going to help her get a Job. It was such a nice re-union. To my disappointment, Mac said that he could not go out with Maria because she was too fat, and that he preferred slim girls like Tessy. I told him not to even think about Tessy.

"Come on Tom, I didn't say I prefer Tessy, I said the likes of Tessy and there are a million and one girls out there that are like Tessy, you know it was as if I walked into AM Express, Tessy looks so much like Mariam"

"Mariam?

"Yes, the cute presenter on AM Express"

"Oh, yes, they have the same complexion and she had the same hairstyle"

"Yes"

"You know my greatest expectation in life?"

"No"

"It's to see her in another hair style; I can give anything for that"

"To see who?"

"What do you mean who? Mariam of course"

"Oh and how is her hair style your business?"

"I am her fan… I am just tired of that hair style, I want to see her wearing long tiny braids or dreads or even afro…"

Chapter 9

A FTER TWO MONTHS of job hunting, I finally discovered that there was vacancy at the Accounts department right in my dad's company.

I called Tessy asked her to come down and got a place for her to stay. A week later she arrived. When I told her about the job she was over excited. I asked her to send in her application the next day.

I got home to find my mum very angry "what's wrong mum?"

"Its your sister Yvonne, she went out since afternoon and its almost ten p.m now"

"Mother she's twenty one, I think she's matured enough to take care of herself"

"Tom I know she's matured but since this holidays, she has not been staying at home at all. On Wednesday she lied to me that she was going to see her friend Queen, when it was nine p.m I called Queen's house only to discover that she never went there, Queen even traveled out for the holidays and that got me concerned".

"But why would she lie?" I asked

"That's what I don't know, she'll be writing her exams in two months, I expect her to be reading her books and not roaming about. Please Tom talk to her, if your father ever finds out, he'll send her away..."

"Alright mum I will"

We waited for Yvonne, until ten thirty p.m. She was shocked to find us in the sitting room

"Mummy I'm sorry, I called the house twice but could not get through"

"And where do you think you're coming from?" I asked. She started laughing,

"Hey Tom, you sound exactly like daddy, anyway I went out with my boy friend" Then she waved her finger at us "he asked me to marry him" I didn't know what to say. My mum jumped up.

"Let me have a look" she said, "oh this ring is beautiful, it is a sapphire, this must have cost him a fortune."

"Yvonne who is this boy friend of yours"

"Fiancé" corrected my mum.

"Whatever" I replied, "who is he and how come you've never brought him to the house?"

"I wanted it to be a surprise"

"Mummy, this is not right, how could he just ask her to marry him when he has not met anyone of us, Yvonne I am so disappointed in you, You've made yourself so cheap".

"Come on Tom, he's not marrying us but Yvonne, they didn't want to involve anybody, its so romantic, he loves her for who she is, he is not interested in her background but her, so Yvonne when and how did you meet him".

"Mummy it's a long story, I've known him for some time now but we started going out recently"

"Where does he work?"

"He works in a company" she replied, "oh mummy I'm so happy and tired. I'll just take a shower and rest good night". She was obviously avoiding my questions I was angry at the way my mum was taking things so lightly.

"Tom, I'm very happy for her, at least I'll start planning my Child's wedding for the first time in my life. You have refused to get married and your younger sister is ready to take the bold step don't you feel green?"

"Mummy she is a lady, it's not fair that you are comparing us"

"I'm sorry I can't help but compare, you are nine years older than she is"

"Mummy my time will come I've not just found the right person"

"You don't even have a girl friend, well I don't care if you decide to become a monk because I am not waiting for you to give me grandchildren. I already have three and now Yvonne is also getting married. I'm so proud of her. God knows how hard I've longed for this..." Suddenly she was in another world

"Goodnight mum" I said and left, she didn't even notice my departure. The next morning at the office I told Mac about my day with Tessy and about Yvonne's engagement.

He laughed, "Tom you should be happy your little sister is getting married, I wish Kate would get married too"

"Mac you don't understand, we don't even know the guy, can you imagine? He sneaks around with her behind our backs".

"Come on, Tom, he might be the shy type that doesn't like showing his face until everything is certain".

"Certain, in what way? I have a feeling that he wants to use her and dump her. I'm sure he's already using her. She comes home late at night and the idiot does not even have the decency of bringing her into the house, he drops her at the gate and zooms off. You understand, he has no respect for us, I can't wait to lay my hands on him"

"Come on Tom you are taking this personal..." after chatting a while I remembered I had to go and pick my dad from the airport.

"Mac I have to go and get daddy from the airport and Tessy's coming, please show her where to submit her application, and tell her to wait for me in my office,"

"She should wait for you in your office all by herself?"

"Do you have a better idea where she should wait?" I asked.

"Of course, she could wait in my office, don't tell me that you don't trust me"

"I trust you Mac, it's just that I know you'll be busy…"

Tom the way you shield Tessy away from me might just make me curious, don't push me to want to find out more about her" I could not believe my ears

"Mac you are out of your senses if you go near Tessy I'll kill you"

Tom you know I love people threatening me it brings out the goal getter in me"

"Alright I'm sorry if you feel threatened, it's just that I think I love Tessy, please stop fantasizing about her"

"Tom I know how scared of girls you are. I know you hate women"

How do you feel when you see my scars? Don't you get scared of women as well? I think Tessy is different…"

"Tom don't mind me you are running out of time but trust me with Tessy, No stupid Woman can come between us"

"You are right my guy"

I picked my dad from the airport and he was very pleased to see me. He hugged me so tight that I could not breathe. He went for his routine checkup. He confided in me that his blood pressure was fluctuating so he had to slow things down. He also complained of attacks of Angina pectoris a major symptom of stroke. He told me that he had to retire completely.

"Oh Tom, what would I have done without you? Who would have continued from where I'm stopping now?" As I drove him home, I told him everything that happened at home and at the office; of course I didn't tell him about Yvonne even though it nearly came out through my mouth, I had to swallow it back. About the Accounts department, he said.

"We might not employ new hands yet auditors have to come in to check books and balances. I want a new accounts department. I've bought some computers, which will arrive next week; it might take another two to three months before the accounts department comes alive again. Meanwhile place adverts and start scrutinizing applications ok".

"All right dad"

I didn't know what to tell Tessy, I knew she'd be frustrated having to wait for another two to three months. That evening I explained things to her over dinner. To my surprise she was excited, oh Tom, it's lovely, and I'll be able to run a computer course. With computer literacy I know I'll stand a better chance" That night I slept beautifully.

The next weekend was my dad's retirement ceremony as well as my promotion. I became the managing director of the company.

As managing director, every decision had to be approved by me so every evening I would go to my dad's room and discuss things with him then, he would advise me on what to do.

After three weeks we organized an aptitude test for all the applicants. They were up to a hundred while we needed just nine people!

I got home one evening to discover that my dad had a heart attack! I could not believe it. He was hospitalized for two weeks so I had to shuttle between hospital, office and home. No one could explain my dad's sudden heart attack. He was a happy man, besides he had just come from his routine medical checkup and everything seemed all right. My mum was the most affected. She obviously didn't want to become a widow too soon.

"Tom is there any problem, at the company?" my mum inquired as she walked me to the car.

"Problem? What kind of problem?"

"Is the company having financial problems?"

"No mum, there's no such thing, why did you ask?"

"It's just that the lawyer and a guy look some files to him that day he had the heart attack. Shortly after they left, Chioma went to his room and found him collapsed on the floor. I just have a feeling that the lawyer and that guy gave him bad news. Tom I want you to find out from the lawyer what transpired that day okay?"

"Yes mum, I think you're right, his heart attack was due to shock and something must have caused that shock," I said thoughtfully.

"Tom I'll also like you to check the company let's know if anything is wrong there okay?"

"Alright mum, I'll do just that" I admired my mum. It was so thoughtful of her. I went to Mr. Alexander's house immediately I left the office. He was very surprised to see me. He avoided my eyes and made the conversation very short. Could he be hiding anything from me?

"Yes Tom, we were with your dad but there was nothing really serious we discussed".

"Mr. Alexander, I'll like to know what you talked about"

"Look Tom, I'm your father's lawyer and anything we talk about is strictly confidential besides that day we were three. I don't discuss serious issues with a third party around".

"Who was this third party?" I asked

"Honestly Tom, I don't know him, someone brought him to me that he wanted to see your dad and I took him to the house"

"Who is this someone that brought him to you?"

"He works for your dad, I don't exactly know what he does but he works for your dad. Look Tom, I have to go somewhere right now, extend my love to your mum" Before I could say anything he grabbed his car keys and rushed out of the house. I could not imagine where he was going to in his jeans and singlet. He wasn't even putting on slippers!

As I drove home I kept wondering. It was obvious that Mr. Alexander was not saying the whole truth and the way he ended the conversation was... Perhaps he was still ashamed of himself, I smiled remembering the incidence with Chioma. When I got home I explained everything that transpired between Mr. Alexander and I to my mum.

"I knew it she said, my spirit never lies to me. Tom there's more to it, I know that there's more to it"

"I think so too mum".

"Remember when Happy was kicked out of the house? Mr. Alexander was the one that brought those files for your dad. I've never stopped wondering how your dad got the information about happy, I asked him on several occasion and he would not tell me, there's something sinister about that lawyer Tom, I can swear it". I agreed with my mum completely. We decided to keep an eye on the lawyer. As my mum was about to leave for the hospital that night, Yvonne came home crying hysterically.

"What's the problem dear?" Inquired my mum "this can't be happening to me" Yvonne said. To be sincere with you I hate women that cry. I hate tears.

"Look Yvonne, stop behaving like a baby and tell us what happened to you" I demanded but she continued crying.

"Mummy you'll be late, she's not ready to tell us what happened"

"No Tom, let me find out, Yvonne, was your purse snatched away from you?"

"No" she replied

"Oh my God, it has happened" mummy cried "oh! Jesus, it can't be true, it can't be true"

"What can't be true?" I asked. "Will both of you tell me what's happening?"

"I think your father is dead"

"Yvonne" I shouted. "Is daddy dead?" I was on the verge of tears myself.

"No no", Yvonne cried, "daddy is all right"

"Then what's the problem Yvonne?" my mum demanded wiping away her tears.

"You got me so afraid. Are you sure your dad is okay?"

"Yes mum, he's very okay, the doctor even said that he'll be discharged in two days," Yvonne said so I stopped panicking.

"I've spoken to Happy's husband and he has convinced Happy to allow their sons come over for a while, I'm sure your dad will be happy to meet them at home when he's discharged" "that's so thoughtful of you mum" I said smiling.

"But Tom you'll have to go to Abuja to get them"

"No problem mum, I'll leave tomorrow"

"Now Yvonne, are you ready to tell us what happened?"

"Mummy, my fiancé jilted me, he said we cannot get married anymore"

"What!" exclaimed my mum. I busted out with laughter

"Mummy what did you expect? Did you think that someone with good intentions would be hiding from us?"

"My God" said my mum "what is becoming of this world?"

"Yvonne I would like you to take me to his house tomorrow I have to see his parents"

"For what" I asked "I am sure his parents know nothing about Yvonne he just wanted a fling and he got one, I told you Yvonne but you wouldn't listen"

I left them angrily. Mummy was wasting her time comforting Yvonne...

The next day after seeing my dad at the hospital, I left for Abuja to bring my nephews. When my dad got home and met his grandchildren he became very happy. Joy, happiness and fulfillment were written all over his face. We were sure that he was going to remain healthy for a very long time.

Chapter 10

A FTER THE APTITUDE test we invited the fifteen best scorers for the interview but we needed just nine people. I knew the interview was going to be tough because all of them were very good. The board of directors', which I was a part of, had to carry out the interview. Tessy of course was one of the best fifteen. I didn't want her to be taken on my recommendation so I allowed things flow naturally. It was the first time in my life that I would be part of an interview panel and it was an exciting experience.

It was Tessy's turn to answer questions...

"How do you intend to move the accounts department forward if you eventually become the head of department?"

"I'll do my job to the best of my ability and even more by so doing the department will definitely move forward," she answered

"What about bankruptcy?"

Another person asked, "companies go into bankruptcy overnight, no one sees it coming, not even its head of accounts, how do you intend to check this?"

"Bankruptcy is a very relative term, what this company sees as bankruptcy may not be seen as bankruptcy in another company but, there's a general cause of bankruptcy which is not checking or curbing excesses. As head of accounts, curbing all excesses will be my watch word".

That was my Tessy, she gave them all the right answers, the next person was the best. He scored ninety eight percent in the aptitude test! It was as if he had the questions before hand also there was something sinister about him...

I watched him closely. he was roughly dressed. I looked at him from head to toe and to my amazement he wore slippers! I could not contain my anger so I attacked him outright.

"Mr. Martins, do you consider this interview serious?" I asked, he looked at me straight in the eye and answered, "Yes I do". "Then why are you dressed like this, do you realize that your shabby dressing could disqualify you?"

"No" he replied, "I had no idea that my dressing could disqualify me"

"I personally think that you are not serious, I mean how could you wear slippers for an interview".

"This is not an ordinary slippers" he replied, "It is a palm slippers!"

Everyone laughed. Believe me the guy was something else. He was very rude. Questions were thrown at him...

"You have a diploma in Accounts and Audit, then a degree in marketing, where do you think you could function best".

"I will function best in Account. You see the head of accounts department should have a sound knowledge of audit, this will go a long way in making sure that both internal and external auditors are well in check"

"You might know much about account and audit but the advert clearly stated that only those with a degree in Accounting need apply, who short-listed him for the aptitude test? Who short-listed him for the aptitude test?" I repeated angrily. "This is what happens when we do not stick to rules..."

Dele cut me short, "I was born an Accountant, I eat accounts, sleep accounts and talk accounts. After my diploma I could not get admission to read accounting because I had no connections. I knew no one. I had no money to bribe. I had no parents, my dad abandoned me and my mum died when I was ten. I had to push trucks to pay my fees. Most of you don't know how hard it is to bring up oneself". I broke the silence that followed as everyone kept staring at him.

"Mr. Martins, that was very touching but not a soul here is interested in your life history okay, get out of here this minute."

He left banging the door behind him. We were all lost for words and I broke the silence again

"Who short-listed Dele Martins for the aptitude test?" I asked clasping my fist angrily on the table. No one answered,

"Ladies and gentlemen, am I not talking to someone? These people were getting on my nerves, with the bulk of work I had to do, scrutinizing all the application thoroughly wasn't just possible, did they expect me to do everything around here? It was then that I understood what my dad meant when I was a kid "... Tom, I manage the company, I oversee everything the people, the money the asset..." so this is what overseeing everything is all about...

"Actually", said Mrs. John interrupting my thoughts. "I handled that part Mr. Davies, but I didn't personally short-list him".

"Are you trying to say that no one invited him for the aptitude test?"

"Actually, the applications were so much that em, I could not go through each one"

"Oh, how lovely Mrs. John." I said sarcastically. What a lazy woman I thought. The sight of Mrs. John believe me would give any man that had blood flowing through his veins tachycardia, such a beauty but no brains. Why on earth did God waste such a beautiful body!

"Are you saying that you just closed your eyes and picked up..."

"No, No Mr. Davies I didn't do that" she cut in

"Actually the computer short-listed Dele martins I programmed it, you know, to reduce the bulk of work and all that, I think I have the program right here", she brought it out of her brief case and passed it to me "so this is not my fault but the computer's"

"Who programmed the computer?" I inquired throwing the paper back at her.

Other members of the board didn't utter a word as usual. I just wished that they would at least make a comment. At first, their silence made me nervous but my dad advised me to take no interest in what their faces looked like because they had all trained themselves to hide their feelings from their face. Shakespeare was right when he said that 'you cannot judge the appearance of the heart from the face' I had to tackle the issue the way a normal managing director would but...

I decided to speak my own mind "ladies and gentlemen, I guess we're through here, it's obvious that Dele martins can't head the accounts department..."

"No" replied Mrs. Agift

I stared at her horrible fat face "what did you say Mrs. Agift" I asked

"You heard me right Mr. Davies, this guy is good, we need stuff like him, he scored ninety eight percent in the test for God sake lets..."

"No Mrs. Agift" said Mr. Rafel. "The guy has a kind of inferiority complex I don't think he'll be any good to us".

"Ladies and gentlemen I said, I can understand now that we all are not of one mind we have a divided house. Therefore we'll put it to vote. We'll meet in two days.

Everyone left me in the boardroom. I was furious, how could Mrs Agift and the other fools see anything in Dele Martins? It was either Dele or Tessy for the post, one of them had to lose and it was definitely not going to be Tessy.

After five minutes I stood up and dragged myself to my office. To my surprise I found Tessy in my office! She looked pale and was staring into space that she didn't even hear me come in.

"Tessy" I gently called out to her and she jumped right out of her skin, and fell down on the rug.

"Tom, I didn't hear you come in," she said trying to get up but the extension wire hooked her leg and she fell down. I quickly threw my briefcase on the sofa and bent down to help her. I saw tears in her eyes

"Come on Tessy what's wrong with you?" I asked I could not understand why she was crying.

"Tom I'm so hungry, I've not eaten anything since yesterday"

"Why?" I asked surprised, "why should you hunger strike?"

"I'm not hunger striking Tom, it's just that I am flat broke"

"Broke?"

I could not picture Tessy broke, silly of me not to have a clue that she was facing any difficulties. Tears were still flowing down her cheeks. Crying ladies always, make me remember Angela...

I gathered her into my arms and wiped away her tears, with words of comfort. Before I knew what I was doing I was kissing her and she was responding perfectly. It was the first time in the five years that I'd known Tessy that something like that would happen between us. We continued kissing each other so hungrily, it was as if Tessy was going to eat my mouth. That made me, realize how hungry she was. Suddenly my door was flung wide open and Dele Martins came in, we hurriedly disengaged but the harm had already been done, he had seen us kissing!

"You idiot" I screamed at him, "don't you know how to knock".

"I am sorry, I didn't know that you are very busy, perhaps I should come back later" he replied and turned to walk away

"Come back later for what?" I asked.

"For some things we have to get straight between each other" he replied

"Some things like what?"

"I repeat that the environment is not conducive, I mean you are in the middle or should I say the beginning of something really serious so I'll excuse you, but I'll call in the next one hour or there about. Enjoy yourselves" he replied and walked away banging the door behind him.

Dele Martins come into my office without knocking! "Where is that skinny secretary of mine?" I summoned her via the intercom

"Tessy, I'm so sorry, I apologize for the embarrassment I've caused you…"

"Here I am sir," said my secretary

"Why did you allow that lunatic enter my office like that?"

"I'm sorry sir, he said you were expecting him right away"

"I guessed as much, not just a lunatic but also a liar. Look Joy, don't ever allow him into my office okay?"

"Alright sir, I'm very sorry sir"

"No problem, don't just allow it happen in the future and please call the canteen or wherever you know would be fastest and order for our lunch. You know my favorite"

"I do sir"

"Thank you and please we are starving"

"Right away sir"

That was my secretary, her middle name was efficient with a capital E, she made life at work very easy for me, all my activities were kept well documented and I'm reminded three times before the day of any appointment. She understood me perfectly.

"So Tessy, I apologize again for the embarrassment I caused"

"Come on Tom, it wasn't embarrassing to me as much as it was for you so I should be the one apologizing"

"Tessy I really enjoyed kissing you"

"Really?" she asked

"Yes, I don't know why it took me so long, for the past five years I've been watching your beautiful lips." she could not look at me anymore.

"Tess, I know you know that I've always loved you"

"I had no idea", she replied

"Tessy I didn't want to rush you into a relationship while you were still at the University because I didn't want to distract your attention from your studies, but I guess that right now is a perfect time for us to start a relationship"

"I don't know" she replied. Our lunch arrived. We ate silently at the inner room.

"Tom what's wrong with Dele Martins?"

"I wish I knew Tess, I have no idea"

"He's got nerves," Tessy said

"Yes Tess, more nerves than anyone can ever imagine"

"Tessy, do you em... I mean are you seeing anyone now?"

"No I'm not"

"Tell me about the guys you went out with in school"

"I didn't go out with anyone"

"Come on, don't lie to me, a girl as cute as you must have lots of toasters and must have fallen for one or two guys"

"Must have fallen prey to one or two guys you mean" she replied.

"Prey?"

"Yes Tom, prey, and don't tell me that you don't know what girls are for in UI.

"Hmmm" I replied. "I guess I do," remembering all the prey I captured in those days.

"So are you saying that you've never gone out with anyone?"

"No" she replied, "I've gone out with someone"

"Someone?" I asked, "Just one person?"

"Tom, you're making me nervous, why all these questions?"

"Curiosity I guess"

'Alright I've gone out with more than one person, what about you Tom?"

"In those days", I replied smiling, "when I was in the world" she laughed "I had many of them but I gave them up."

"That's what everybody at University of Ibadan kept wondering, why did you give up girls Tom?"

"Hmm, how do I explain it to you Tess?" I could not tell her the truth and I didn't what to lie to her either then I thought of the scars, it occurred to me that she was going to see the scars one day so I told her the truth.

"You see em..."

"Out with it Tom"

"Alright, alright Tess I hope you won't hold it against me, because I don't want you to have a bad opinion of me, but I want you to know everything about me, the clean and the dirty"

She nodded "of course Tom, I know that old things are past away"

"That's my girl" I said then I told her everything. She could not believe it "Tom, it's a sad story but you sure did learn your lesson"

"Tessy, I nearly lost my life to learn my lesson what if I had become sterile?"

The phone rang, I picked it up and it was Dele Martins again

"What do you want?" I inquired

"I hope you enjoyed yourself, don't tell me that I quenched the fire that was burning between the two of you"

"Of course we enjoyed ourselves you Idiot, what exactly do you want from me?"

"Nothing" he replied. "I just want you to know that I am the new head of Accounts department"

"Congratulations" I retorted and hung up

"Who was that?" Tessy inquired

"An associate" I replied. I called Mac and his secretary told me he was out. Tessy and I talked for a while. I made sure that she said yes to a relationship before I let her go. I had so much work to do so I could not go shopping with her. I gave her money and asked my driver to take her. She was so grateful that she kissed me good night so passionately before she left. I settled down to work and worked until five p.m then called Mac's office again, Mac didn't come back after lunch I was told. I decided to go to his house as there was a lot to tell him. I got to his house and was relieved to find him. I told him everything about the interview and Dele Martins behavior. Mac became infuriated

"How dared he" Mac screamed, "I'm sure he is not serious about getting the job else I see no reason why he would step on the big boss toes"

"Mac everything about the guy is sinister, you need to see how rough he appeared during the interview in slippers".

"Jees, I would have sent him out but of course Tom, he cannot get the job whatever other members of the board think"

"There'll be an election Mac, I won't have the final say"

"Then see them one after the other and convince them, it's called lobbying, let them really understand that the guy has wings. So what if he got ninety eight percent in the aptitude test believe me Tom, he must have used Juju if not tell me where he got this extreme confidence from"

"Beats me Mac, honestly, my blood runs cold anytime I see him, I hate to say this Mac but I hate him. I just know that I can never work with him. But how do I meet them one after the other, Mac that will not do good to my rep"

"Then I suggest that you see your dad, tell your dad everything, I know he'll be able to convince them"

"I know that too Mac, but it's just that these days my dad shuts me out of his life"

"Shuts you out? How and why would he do such a thing?"

"I don't know Mac, it's just this feeling of coldness and rejection I feel whenever I am with him. Whenever I enter his room he's sleeping"

"Come on, how would a sleeping man reject you?"

"That's it Mac, he pretends to be asleep, it's like he does not want any type of discussion with me anymore. Those days he would wait and ask me about things at the office but now…I don't know how to explain it to you Mac"

"I guess I cannot understand because you cannot explain. However I suggest that you wake him up from his sleep and tell him everything, look at you Tom, you are saying he's shutting you out, he might also be feeling that you are shutting him out".

I nodded. I was the one wearing the shoe so I guess just I would forever know where it hurts.

"So wake your dad up from whatever sleep or pretext to sleep and tell him your problem"

I nodded again, and then took my leave. Mac saw me off to my car, as we got to their car pack which was well illuminated; I noticed the bruises on Mac's cheeks.

"Mac what's on your cheeks?"

"Oh!" he exclaimed touching it "this, so you've not noticed it since?"

"Since when?" I asked

"I can't remember exactly when, some silly electric ants did stuffs to me".

"But Mac, it's looking like fresh cuts"

"Looking fresh?" he asked touching it again "I guess I'll have to go and look at it in the mirror"

We said good-byes and I left. I got home to meet my mum in tears.

"What happened?" I asked

"It's your sister Tom, she tried to kill herself".

"What!"

"Yes Tom, I was sitting down right here when she came back in tears. I asked her where she was coming from and why she was crying, she said she went out with that fiancé of hers that jilted her and they had a fight. Of course I hissed and went to my room, what else could I do? I've tried to get the guy's address from her to talk some sense into him but she would not give me any information. Tom I nearly lost a daughter because I did not care about her enough I am such a bad mother, I've failed to bring up my children the way I ought to"

"Come on mum you cannot continue to say such things about yourself, you know it's not your fault". She continued "After a while, Chioma rushed in to inform me that Yvonne tried to kill herself by hanging she was already choking to death when Chioma got there. My only wish now is finding that guy because she was going through hell because of him.

I was lost for words. I didn't feel sorry for Yvonne but my mum. How could a girl as young and beautiful as Yvonne attempt suicide because of a man? I wondered what my dad would do if he heard about it. "Things have gone out of hand because we did not tell daddy about it from the start" I said to myself, Yvonne needed someone stronger to contend with and I was definitely going to tell my dad about it. Maybe this would break the thick wall that had formed between us.

Chapter 11

TOO NUMEROUS FRIENDS were one thing I never had in my entire life, but the very few friends I had were jealously guarded. I didn't need the whole world to be by my side to feel happy but the few people I had made me very happy and contented. You can therefore imagine the level of emptiness I feel when the very few people in my life start misbehaving.

My dad was finally diagnosed as having a terminal ailment so he had to await death on the bed.

I realized that my dad was avoiding me because of an incidence that occurred. I had gone to see him and as usual his eyes were shut and he was snoring. I left feeling he was truly sleeping; as I strolled downstairs I met the lawyer, Mr. Alexander on his way up.

"Good evening Mr. Alexander daddy is fast asleep I'm afraid"

"But Chioma just called to tell him I'm here and he said I should come up right away"

"Alright" I said and he went upstairs. I didn't want to argue with him because I knew he was going to meet daddy fast asleep.

After a while I had to go upstairs because Mr. Alexander had not come down. I went to the room and eaves dropped. I also peeped through the keyhole to behold my dad chatting and laughing with all tenacity. I knocked the door and entered the room, immediately I entered my dad's countenance changed.

"Tom why don't you come back later" he snapped, "Mr. Alexander and I are discussing something really serious, thank you," he said dismissively.

I could not believe that my dad would do such a thing. In the past he would tell me 'sit down and join us Tom, you know I cannot hide anything from you' but the same person asked me to leave...

The rejection hit me so much that I got a bottle of wine and went to my room to calm down. Since that day the battle line was drawn between my dad and I. once in a while I would go and see him but as usual his eyes were always closed and he never asked to see me.

The problem with Dele Martins was consuming me. I knew I had to tell daddy about it because I could not approach the board of directors' one on one.

I went to his room three times. I would get to the door and the courage to face him would fail me.

I tried calling his cell phone but I changed my mind and called Tessy instead. We talked for an hour after which she invited me over to her place for dinner.

I took a shower got dressed and prepared to go to Tessy's for dinner and decided I would see my dad when I got back home. Chioma knocked my door, as I was about to open it.

"Tommy, your dad wants to see you"

Saying I was shocked would be a tremendous understatement. I could simply not believe it

"Chioma are you sure?" I inquired

"Of course I'm sure, and he said you should come right away"

I did go right away, I could not just believe my luck. I realized that I was shaking and was really nervous. I knocked and opened the door after he told me to come in. To my surprise he was sitting down at his reading table and writing. But he didn't look excited or happy to see me as he usually does. He stared at me as if I was entirely a new being. Strange is the best word to describe the cold stares he dished out to me.

"How are you feeling, dad?"

"I'm fine, I actually want you to do something for me"

"Just name it dad"

"Actually it's about someone called Dele Martins"

I could not believe it

"Daddy you know Dele Martins?"

"Yes Tom, I do"

"Thank God, I also wanted to talk to you about him. Daddy that guy has been giving me headache and I sincerely do not know how to handle him, he even threatened..."

"Tom please, I didn't call you here to listen to complaints, whatever Dele has done to you I beg of you to forgive him because he has to get that job"

"What do you mean dad, why..."

"Exactly what I just said, I suggest you start getting along with him"

"You cannot be serious, daddy we have a policy at the company which I intend to follow"

"Look Tom, I actually owe his dad a lot and I feel that the job will you know..."

"I don't know anything anymore dad, you've changed suddenly where for God's sake did I go wrong? Daddy where is that trust you once had in me? Why do you antagonize..."

"Tom I will not argue with you, I have made my decision and that's final"

"Daddy Dele Martins gets the job over my dead body, not as long as I remain the managing director"

"Tom I am a major shareholder in the company, I decide who remains managing director and you know it"

"Oh... I had no idea" I said sarcastically "Dele Martins could as well become the managing director because I quit"

I left his room angrily banging the door behind me; I got my car keys and drove straight to Mac's house forgetting some basic rules of driving:

Do not drive when you're very upset.

Do not drive under the influence of alcohol as these could divide your attention and steal away concentration.

Chapter 12

D<small>ON'T WORRY</small> I didn't have a serious accident. Well it totally depends on your idea of what a serious accident should be like. For instance running into a wall, running into a river or running into a human being are all different forms of collision but believe me some people would rather run into a human being than run into a wall. Reason is that a human being would not dent their cars as much as a wall would. Let me tell you a secret some men cherish their cars more than their wives, girlfriends, kids and what have you. They call their cars names like baby, sweetie... going back to my accident, no I didn't run into a river or a wall and I wouldn't have preferred running into a human being because I wasn't using my baby, anyways I ran into a lesser form of a human being_ an animal. I ran into a very stubborn goat, it wasn't a head on collision I dodged and dodged this goat but we still collided. It was so infuriating the way they all kept shouting at me. I mean they were there and they saw how the silly goat played pranks with me.

Immediately after the accident, they carried the dead goat, put it on top of my car and asked me to pay for it. I could not believe the exorbitant price they asked for claiming that the goat was pregnant and usually gives birth to four kids so I had to pay for five goats!

"Oga, this goat dey born four to five pikin"

"Okay, how much is your money?"

"The money big o"

"If it's too much then I'll have to go and get the money from home"

"Get wetin, look oga, this goat be my hope for life and you don kill am now, I been talk say I go sell all the children wey the goat go born use the money buy car so you go fit just drop your car"

"My car?" I inquired.

"Yes oga, make you drop your car or make you pay one hundred thousand naira or make we go police station choose one"

Going to the police would have been my best option but I wasn't in the mood for any police case. I'd rather spend that cash on these poor individuals. The reason why they were trying to extort money from me was poverty.

I was able to plead and at the end I parted with fifty thousand naira! As I was about to leave they removed the goat from the top of my car. It was not as if I needed the goat but their greed pissed me off, they had the money and still wanted the goat!

I finally got to Mac's house but to my disappointment he wasn't home. I had nowhere to go to. Outside my dad and Mac there was no one else I could go to in times of grief like this.

"Where the hell is Mac," I shouted when I got behind the steering, Mac's mum heard me scream and rushed out.

"Is everything alright Tom?"

"Yes ma"

"Then why were you screaming?" She noticed blood stain all over my car

"Oh my God Tom, you had an accident?"

"Yes ma, but it wasn't serious, I ran into a goat".

"Oh Tom, how terrible, and look any accident is serious, believe me, running into a chicken is also a serious accident"

"I don't think so ma"

"Tom when you run into animals there's always a danger of another car behind you running into you, or you could even drive off the road into a ditch, you understand what I mean".

"I guess I do" I replied

"Why don't you come in and have a drink with me while Ali cleans your car"

"I don't think so ma"

"Come on Tom, the police might frustrate you if they see your car like this"

That did the trick. I didn't want any encounter with the police so I decided to have the drink with Mac's mum.

We talked for thirty minutes, I mean she talked for about thirty minutes because I just sat down there giggling and laughing as I wasn't even hearing anything that she was saying. The next thing, she was frowning at me.

"I cant believe this Tom, what's got into you, I'm telling you that Kate had a serious crisis yesterday and you're laughing".

"I am very sorry ma, actually I thought you said that Kate was coming back home how is she doing now?"

"She's still in the hospital. Donald has gone to be with her".

"I'm so sorry ma, don't worry nothing will happen to her"

"Tom, I don't know but no one speaks about Kate with such conviction I just feel relieved Tom, I know she'll make it". I felt flattered but jees she made it sound as if I was God, the one to finally say its over before Kate dies. I excused myself and called Mac's mobile phone again but could still not get to him.

"There's still no reply?" She inquired

"Yes ma"

"Tom, I don't know what's wrong with Mac, he's been coming home late for some time now, I was wondering where you guys always go to after work".

"I have no idea ma, why don't you ask Mac where he goes to."

"Ask Mac? Tom, you want me to question the movements of a guy that is over thirty years old?" I didn't know what to say, why then was she questioning me?

"Tom, from the time you were a little boy you've been very understanding and have always displayed a level of maturity which I admire, believe me I was very grateful to God when I saw how close you and Mac became"

"Thank you ma, but I don't think I understand why you are saying all these" I mean she didn't have to flatter me to get information about Mac from me.

"What I am saying is that, you and Mac should settle down, you guys go out after work doing whatever you always do" I could not believe my ears because Mac and I had no time for outings during the week.

"It's only on Saturdays we actually spend time together, playing, basketball right here in this house" I replied.

"I know you spend Saturdays together but are you trying to tell me that you know nothing about Mac's whereabouts?"

"Cross my heart. I am surprised you are saying all these and tell me would I be looking for him if I knew where he was?"

"You are right Tom, but tell me, when do you guys intend to settle down?"

"Very soon"

"Then I'll like to meet your girlfriends, bring them to the house, on Saturday, invite them over to play basketball with you guys"

"That's a very nice suggestion, but I'm afraid it won't be possible."

"Why?"

"They work on Saturdays"

I had to end the conversation. Somehow Mac was becoming mysterious. I remembered the bruises on his face and wondered if he was involved with some cultists or if he was doing drugs…

I finally said goodnight to Mrs. Donald. Getting up from the hot seat that she put me left my butt aching. I could not understand why Mrs. Donald would worry about Mac that much. It wasn't as if we could not afford our own apartment, but we decided that staying with our parents would shield us from temptation.

I wanted so much to go to a nightclub but the goat incidence left me broke, so I had to go back home to get some money. I rushed to my room and got some money but unfortunately for me I met my mum in the sitting room on my way out. Damn!

"Oh Tom, I'm so happy that you are back. Chioma told me about the misunderstanding and how you went out drunk. Thank God you're back safely and what exactly were you guys arguing about" I told her everything.

"Tom your father is passing through a phase in his life right now. He told me to my face that he doesn't want to see me for the rest of his life"

"You don't say," I replied really surprised, "Why would he say such a thing?"

"I have no idea Tom, but hear this; he has been calling Happy and begging her to forgive him"

That got me really surprised I had to just keep listening so I didn't utter a word.

"He calls her twice everyday but you know how stubborn Happy could be, she has refused to come and see him, her husband said he is persuading her to come anyway".

"Mummy, why didn't you ever say anything? I can imagine the trauma you're going through because I'm going through the same thing. What I don't understand is why just the two of us?"

"It beats me too, maybe it's because we are the ones that he loves most. It's like his emotions changed, those he loved so much he now hates and happy that he loathed so much is now his love"

"But he doesn't hate Yvonne, he still loves her how do we explain that?" I asked.

"I didn't even think about Yvonne" she replied "anyway I've read and asked experts at the hospital about his condition and gathered that it's quite a normal psychological response for people having terminal ailments. We are not to react angrily but to keep showering him with love and attention for instance I send him love notes every morning. Tom please honor his request, if you refuse or quit you'll end up worsening his condition"

"But mum Dele martins has been throwing his weight around, he even went as far as telling me that no matter what he would get the job..."

"I know Tom, but sometimes it's good we remain cowards because of people we love, and I know how much you love your dad so please do this for him okay?"

"Do you know anything about a friend of dads' called Mr. Martins?"

"I have never heard of him" she replied

"You see mum, that's my problem, I've also never heard about him, if daddy really owes him so much we ought to know him, he must have mentioned him somehow"

"You are right Tom, a lot of things are going wrong, I'm still having some cranky feelings about that lawyer" then she paused, both of us were deep in thoughts. She broke the silence, "Tom we have to pray, its only God that can help us, this is not a time for you to play around and drink, this is a time to enter into a serious warfare for I do not think that we are wrestling against flesh and blood. Get on your knees my son. Let's sink everything up in prayers. I feel that something awful is about to happen to us, I don't know, I just feel somehow, this premonition"

"Don't worry mum, nothing terrible is going to happen to you or anyone else". We said goodnight and went to bed. Talking to her alone had a way of calming me down. I kept wondering what my dad's problem was, why the sudden change of attitude towards my mum and I? Could it be that he discovered what my mum did during my ailment? Or was he insane considering the fact that he had been calling Happy. Perhaps he wanted to make up with her before finally kicking the bucket.

I glanced at the time and it was already twelve midnight, the lust for alcohol was gone but I could not find sleep so I decided to find Mac. I picked the phone to call Mac only to hear the most terrible disappointment in my life. Yvonne was on the line sobbing and pleading. She was doing the most horrible thing a woman would do for a man. She had no pride left for her and damn, take a woman's pride or self esteem away from her and she's nothing but trash in the sight of a man. Sorry in the sight of a man like me, I hate girls that do such things and I started hating Yvonne. The stupid boyfriend of hers just kept sighing, I was so disappointed in Yvonne that I could not even drop the phone; I was just fixed to the spot.

"...Please darling, you can't just say it's over because it is not, I love you and I know you love me too, why do you want to kill me? I swear, I cannot continue life without you, without you there'll be no sun in my sky, there'll be no love in my life, there'll be no life left for me, and I... baby I don't know what I will do I'll be lost if I lost you, if you ever leave baby you'll take away everything.... hey baby I'm very sorry for the way I behaved. I've been taking sleeping pills these days. When you called me to meet you at the restaurant I became myself again, I thought you were going to apologize for breaking the relationship and ask me out all over again. But you dashed all my hopes by saying you are happy that we are still friends. I felt very sad and reacted violently, I can't still believe that I poured my drink on you and pounced on you like a wild cat. How could I ever be friends with you when the love I feel for you is beyond words....

"Are you still there?" she stopped ranting and waited for a reply, "sweetheart say something I know you are there...."

"Mac please say something"

"Mac?" I asked myself

"Yvonne, I've heard all you've been saying, but all the injuries you inflicted on me has roused so much suspicion, even Tom saw it, I had to lie to him but I saw disbelief in his eyes. Yvonne you can't imagine the discomfiture you've caused me."

"Mac I'm sorry, I don't know what got into me, forgive me"

"Alright, I've forgiven you"

"Is that all you are going to say?"

"What else do you want me to say Yvonne?"

"Are we still going out?"

"Of course we are not, Yvonne I've honestly had enough of you for a lifetime, go take whatever pills you've been taking and go to bed, goodnight"

"You can't hang up on me Mac"

"Just listen Yvonne, I'm hanging up right now" and he did just that. She could not even drop the phone, she started crying, I could not believe it. I dropped the phone completely pissed off.

Chapter 13

I CAN'T STILL REMEMBER how I slept that night but saying my discovery was a shock would be a great understatement. Words cannot express how disappointed I was in my so-called best friend. I woke up in the morning feeling that the phone call was a dream, as I could not just make it a reality. Mac and my little sister no no no, it was simply a bad dream.

I went to the bathroom, shaved and brushed my teeth then went for my breakfast; thoughts of Mac and Yvonne kept disturbing me. Deep down in my heart I knew it was not a dream. I decided to give Yvonne the beating of her life, and it was something I had never done before. Big brothers always beat up their little sisters but this little sister of mine was too little, the age difference was so much that we never had the opportunity of fighting as kids well it's a pity that I was going to beat her up at this time that she's an adult. I took my strongest belt and headed for her room. Of course I didn't knock, I just sneaked into her room, and found her lying down on her bed facing the ceiling as if she was receiving a revelation from it. I saw the bags under her eyes and concluded that she didn't sleep. When she turned and saw me standing by her bed she started weeping.

I looked around her room and hell everything was in total disarray. My little sister was totally nonchalant about life all because of one silly bastard. I could not carry out my mission because I felt sorry for her but all my anger and hostility was transferred to the cause of her pain and anguish, Mac.

I didn't know what to do or say to her because whenever I see crying girls all I remember is Angela... I finally broke the silence.

"Why didn't you tell me that it was Mac?" She jumped right out of her skin in shock and horror

"Who... told you" she stammered

"Does it matter?" I replied.

"Oh Tom I'm so sorry" she continued breaking down into fresh sobs; big mighty tears were rolling down her cheeks.

"Oh Jesus, Tom, I sincerely wanted to tell you but I didn't want to come between you and Mac"

"That's not what I'm talking about, I mean at the beginning, the day he asked you out why didn't you tell me?"

"Actually I wanted to but I didn't know how you'll take it and Mac swore you'll never approve. I wanted the wedding plans to begin before disclosing his identity to you"

"Yvonne, you and Mac have betrayed me."

"I'm very sorry, I feel so ashamed..."

"Why the break up then?"

"Mac actually ended the relationship because of you; he said you threatened to deal with whoever my boyfriend was"

"Hmm" I sighed.

"I could not believe it, just like that he stopped calling me, when I called he told me bluntly that the engagement was over but I could keep the ring, that was when I attempted suicide, Tom I feel ashamed telling you all these"

"You don't have to be ashamed, Mac treated you wrongly and he must pay for it. Yvonne he has to pay for all the sleepless nights he has caused you"

"No, please I don't want the friendship I grew up to find between the two of you destroyed because of me. Tom I will never forgive myself for coming between the two of you. Please pretend you don't know what's happening, I believe things will soon become okay between us again. Tom I know he loves me, I am very sure that he loves me..."

Jeez, she was pathetic, the more she talked the more furious I got, despite all her pleas I didn't flinch. A man's gat to do what he's gat to do and thank God it was a Saturday, normal basketball for Mac and I.

I went downstairs for breakfast but I could not take anything in, because I was so nervous. I took my baby and headed for Mac's house. You are wondering who my baby is right? My baby is my car, and it's not the Mercedes Benz C_ class daddy bought for me on my seventeenth birthday. My baby is the car I went out and bought for myself. If you were ever given a car then you finally bought yours, you'll understand what I'm talking about. I cherished the car my dad gave me, it was my pet but I loved the car I bought for myself. Seeing my baby every morning gave me joy and a sense of fulfillment. Yes do not be surprised for I am that guy I told you about. I cherished my baby much more than anything else...

I drove my baby straight to the court and started warming up, quite unlike me. It took Mac thirty minutes after I had arrived before he could summon up courage to the court, quite unlike him. The situation was kind of like me sending out signals of 'you idiot I know' and Mac sending out signals of 'I know you know, what do we do about it?'

"Tom you're early today"

"Early? I don't think so, it's you who's late" I replied. I noticed the scars still on his cheek. I could not even look at his eye and he could not look at mine either.

"Sorry Tom, I could not call you yesterday, my mum told me about the accident. When I got home it was late and em... I just decided to wait till today; I knew you'll come for basketball so..."

"Hmm" it was so unlike Mac. I now understood why he was avoiding me. He felt that my looking for him was to confront him with his deed.

"Let's start the game' I said. We started the game and for the first time in our lives we played like opponents so seriously that after an hour we were already sweating. We rushed into the house for a cold shower as usual.

As I stood under the shower and the sprinkles of cold water hit my bare skin my gall bladder burst and all pent up emotions inside me was unleashed, Mac too jumped out of his shorts and singlet and joined me in the shower. I turned and gave him the hardest blow I could, he stared at me and his eyes were like 'so you know'

"Now spill it out" I said

"Spill what?" he replied

"You don't know?"

"Yes Tom, I don't know, what was that blow for?" I gave him another blow

"Tom why are you doing this, what's wrong with you?"

"Yes Mac, something is wrong with me, and if you really want to know, I am doing this because you've been fucking my little sister right behind my back, that's what is wrong with me Mac. You dumped her afterwards like a bag of trash, is that fair Mac? Is that a fair thing to do to baby Yvonne?"

"Tom let me explain what happened"

"There's no explanation Mac this is a case of child abuse, I can't believe you could even stoop as low as asking a little girl like that out. God, I thought I knew you"

"Shut up Tom, please hear me out there is a saying that the hen is never too young for the cock..."

I faced the shower and the water sprinkled all over my face, calming me down, Mac continued.

"Tom she jumped on me, I can't explain" I laughed.

"She jumped on you ha, how can a little girl like Yvonne jump on big you. Mac, surely you have the strength to push her off really hard, you can do better than that, that's not a good explanation"

"Tom honestly I wish you saw the way she jumped on me, I am flesh Tom I could not resist, I got carried away. Immediately I got my senses back I ended it but I didn't exactly sleep with her..."

"Why didn't you tell me anything, you made a fool of me. I kept confiding in you but you pretended..."

"I'm sorry Tom, I am really sorry and ashamed of myself"

"Why did you ask her to marry you?"

"I felt that you would not approve of anything except marriage, and then you told me that you were going to deal with whoever it was... I had to take a breather because you were so sad and bitter. She could not understand my plight Tom, sincerely I didn't want to destroy the friendship I have with you and...."

"Because of you, Yvonne attempted suicide, she's not herself anymore, you have no idea how broken she is"

"I don't think so Tom, she just feels the hurt of rejection and I know she'll get over it"

"Get over it?" I could not believe my ears. "How do you expect her to get over it?"

"Look Tom, everyone gets a broken heart once in a lifetime, some stupid people get heart broken more than once, it's just a part of life"

I gave him another blow and pounced on him like a lion, the battle started, from his bathroom then we were inside the bedroom, scattering everything, throwing ourselves all round the room. The noise got to Mac's mum and she rushed down to find out what was happening, immediately she opened the door she closed it again because both of us were naked.

"Mac, Tom, what are you guys doing?" she thought we were playing but the sound of breaking bottles and blows made her realize that it was real.

"If you don't stop this, I'm going to call the police. Get dressed let's talk this over...." All her pleas and warning fell on deaf ears.

We stopped the fight when all the cells in our bodies had become crushed. There was blood everywhere, blood gushing out from our noses, mouths and other injuries sustained. Moving my legs was somehow difficult. I picked my bag, wore my shorts and dashed home. Driving home was a miracle as I was feeling pains everywhere even the tips of my fingers were aching.

Chioma was nonplussed when she saw me entering the house.

"Tom were you attacked by armed robbers?"

"No" I went straight to my room and locked the door behind me.

I went down heavily on my bed; I could not go through life anymore. Later I searched for a defense mechanism to reduce the anxious feelings without addressing the problem, because the problem at hand was simply beyond me. I had to distort reality somehow. After all Sigmund Freud's theory of maladaptive behavior got its basis from defense mechanisms.

I tried denying the situation; I told myself that it was simply not possible that Mac and my dad would ever turn their backs on me. I told myself that it was simply a bad dream, but I could not deny it completely deep down inside me, something kept telling me that it was real and not a dream.

I tried to repress the whole situation, like banish it from my consciousness. That tiny voice which kept telling me that everything was real had to be repressed so that the denial tactic would work, it just had to work. But then I thought of suppression, however suppression required deliberate self-control and self-control was something I didn't have at the moment, I didn't even have a self anymore. I banished the suppression option, repression was far better, if only I could repress everything to a point of amnesia. Yes, developing amnesia would be the best of all the options. I tried developing amnesia but it wasn't possible, why the hell didn't Freud give us mechanisms of developing amnesia!

As everything failed, I decided to be rational as being rational would not only ease my disappointment but also provide an acceptable motive for my behavior, why should I feel sorry for quarreling with Mac? After all he deserved it. How could he just play with my sister's emotions? He had overstepped his bounds and I could not forgive him, my fighting him was justified.

The pain my body was going through became unbearable, I could not flex my muscles, even my fingers ached. I eventually called Chioma who gave me tranquilizers and massaged my body with a really hot liniment. After the treatment from Chioma, I slept. I was woken up after twelve hours by my mum and Chioma, they brought dinner. My body temperature was high, so my mum injected me with a drug and the next thing I was fast asleep again. Finally I woke up on Sunday afternoon! I was so hungry that I rushed to the kitchen. I was feeling better anyway; the drugs I was given had blocked all the pain producing receptors. I met Yvonne in the kitchen also having lunch, she was looking so different; her hair was well was made, she was well dressed and was also smiling!

"Wow" I exclaimed, "who is this pretty damsel in my kitchen"

"It's your sister Yvonne"

"No, this cannot be my sister Yvonne because, Yvonne my sister is upstairs in her room crying her eyes out right now" Yvonne's countenance changed so I decided to go soft with her.

"You are so perfectly dressed, why didn't you go to church?"

"I'm preparing to go back to school; I'll be leaving by three p.m. and its already twelve noon I had a lot to pack"

"I have dealt with Mac"

"I know" she replied, "Mac's mum called"

"I want you to go and concentrate fully on your studies. You'll be a nurse in a few weeks, please don't blow it up, Mac is not worth it".

She was very uncomfortable and she kept looking down into her plate.

"Thank you very much Tom," she said finally looking up,

"I always thought that you were going to kill me when you discover but.... I am really ashamed of myself Tom, I am really sorry"

"Yvonne, Mac claims that you jumped on him"

"Jumped on him?" she cut in surprisingly, "I never did anything like that, he was the one that jumped on me"

"Well" I replied, "I don't understand what you and Mac mean by 'jumping on' but whatever you did with Mac landed you in heartbreak so I suggest you do not repeat such things in the future lest you get another heart break"

"Tom the day I came back from school when you were not feeling fine, remember I went out with Mac"

"Yes" I replied

"That was the day it all started between us. He took me to a nice restaurant where we ate then went shopping at the supermarket. He bought this very nice perfume for me... when I sprayed the perfume on my body; I fell in love with Mac. But honestly I didn't jump on him I didn't know what to do about the way I felt, on many occasions I felt like calling him but I could never summon the courage until I came back from school. He called you but you were not in and I answered the call he said he had missed me and was glad that I am back home for holidays. He invited me for dinner and I accepted, it was an offer I had imagined a million times over, but I didn't show him how happy I was... We had such a nice time that he suggested we have dinner again the next day. I could not believe my luck, of course I accepted but I asked him to meet me at the restaurant because I didn't want you to know and he agreed that you would not welcome the idea, that's how it became a secret love affair. On the third night he asked me out and I accepted, we enjoyed each others company so much that we lost touch with time every time we were together.... That's why I was always coming back late. Next he gave me the engagement ring and proposed marriage, he said he wanted us to get married so that we would be together always... Suddenly he changed his mind claiming that you would never approve of our relationship and didn't want you hurt..."

"Yvonne it's okay, it's all over now at least you are talking about him without tears in your eyes and that's progress" she smiled,

"I just feel relieved now that I've finally brought everything out in the open I feel good Tom, keeping the secret from you was very painful, it's all over, I won't brood over that pig anymore".

"You are right Yvonne, that's what you should think of anytime his memories cross your heart, a terrible pig that eats shit" We both burst out laughing.

My mum and Chioma got back from church and were very pleased to see me back on my feet laughing happily.

'Who did you fight with?" my mum asked as If she didn't know

"No one mum"

"No one? But Mac's mum called to inform me that you guys fought".

I didn't want to sound rude so I just kept quiet; I saw no reason why she would be asking me about something she already knew.

"Tom, its normal to have misunderstandings with friends but the idea of big men like you and Mac fighting like little children is beyond me" She turned to Chioma

"I'm sure they quarreled because of a girl. Friends as close as Mac and Tom could only be separated by daughters of eve, how powerful women are" she and Chioma laughed but Yvonne only smiled as per the daughter of eve that separated Mac and I. That afternoon my mum and I took Yvonne to school. She was very grateful because I didn't tell mummy her little secret.

Chapter 14

I T WAS MONDAY morning again. I sat down in the office feeling very lonely, just me against the world. I thought of Mac, usually every morning I'd either call or he'd call and we'll just say hi to each other. I don't know how to explain it, but the betrayal I felt was something beyond pardon, I was hurting terribly and I realized that I could not tolerate seeing Mac anymore, I had to get him out of the company somehow. It was an irony, I got him in and here I was trying to get him out as well!

Ten a.m was the board meeting where we would choose the new accounts head, I thought of Dele Martins, my dad's wish and my mum's suggestion. I could not just allow Dele Martins have his way but I didn't want my dad unhappy... I was so confused but had to decide right there on my chair what I would do, please myself to displease my dad or displease myself to please my dad...

I finally decided to allow the board of directors make the decision and remain neutral during the voting.

I took a deep breath rested my head on my chair and closed my eyes. This exercise did not relax me, it was then that I remembered my earthly comforter; thoughts of a shot of whiskey got me smiling broadly, but wait a minute do I want to go in there with a smell of whiskey on my breath? I had no other choice but to take the whiskey and then conceal the smell somehow, it wasn't an exactly nice experience but I had to conceal the smell by swallowing some puffs of my perfume. I nearly threw up afterwards.

As I opened the door to go and face the devil in his backyard, Tessy walked into my office, she was looking simply gorgeous and I was very pleased to see her, we ran into each other's arms.

"Tom I am nervous I want to know my fate straight away that's why I came" I kissed her hungrily.

"Oh Tessy I've missed you so much, where have you been" she pushed me away

"Tom what did you have for breakfast?"

"Why are you asking?"

"It's just that your lips and tongue taste somehow weird, oh my stomach, my God…" she cried out. I remembered the puffs of perfume I just swallowed

"Really?" I inquired

"Yes Tom, I feel like throwing up" what was I supposed to do?

Before I could suggest a cup of juice or something sweet, she came! She threw up right on me.

"Oh Tom, I'm sorry, I don't know what's wrong with me, and I don't want you to feel that…"

"Don't worry Tess, now let me clear this mess up okay…"

I lead her to the restroom and we cleaned up, I had to remove my suit and dry it up in front of the air conditioner.

Then I gave her a cup of juice and took one myself, I don't know what happened, its either her vomiting stimulated the vomiting center of my brain or a mixture of whiskey, perfume and orange juice stimulated vomiting. At least I was better than Tess, I ran to the restroom before everything came out of me. Tessy was confused, she wanted to call the doctor but I stopped her, as I alone knew the cause of our vomiting.

"Tessy I've missed you, you know"

"Come on Tom, you saw me on Friday"

"Then I guess I'll have to be seeing you every day" she was pleased

"Tom I've missed you too and won't mind seeing you every day. But, I know I was lonelier than you were"

"No Tess, I was lonelier"

"Come on, you know that's not true you always have Mac"

"Mac is gone Tess"

"Come on Tom I saw Mac just now"

"That's not what I mean; Mac's gone out of my life"

"Why should he go out of your life?"

"We had a misunderstanding"

"About what?" Tessy exclaimed.

"I don't want to talk about it"

"Alright, I won't pry, but if you were really missing me why didn't you call?" She got me there.

"Actually I was very moody and would not make a good company for anyone so I just stayed at home"

"Hmm hmm" she sighed. It was like she didn't believe me. I got up and held out a hand to help her up.

"Look Tess, I honestly missed you," I said looking into her eyes. "Can I ask for a favor?"

"Of course you can"

"Can I kiss you?"

"I don't know" she said, "I don't want us vomiting again"

"I promise you won't vomit"

"Why don't you go for the meeting Tom, I'll be here waiting for you. I'll just remove my skirt and dry it in front of the AC, right now..."

I looked at the time and it was already fifteen minutes after ten.

I wore my suit and dashed out. Realizing that I didn't even think of Tessy throughout the weekend was terrible. Everyone was already seated as I walked into the boardroom. I apologized for coming late and took my seat.

"Let's get on with it," I said when the door was thrown wide open and behold my dad in his pyjamas! I was lost for words and so was every other person. Finally, I was able to open my mouth and what came out was

"Daddy, what are you doing here? You know you're not strong enough to get out of bed"

"Shut up you idiot," he replied

Everyone could not believe it

"I just came to inform you all that Tom is trying to talk you into voting for his girlfriend! I refuse to allow my company degenerate into a love nest, I hope I am communicating"

"Daddy how dare you? "Tessy is not my girlfriend"

"Tell that to the birds" he replied, "Why did you come late for this meeting? Isn't it because you were shamelessly making love with Tessy right in your office?"

"Daddy you are insane" I shouted at him, "how dare you..."

"If you all think I'm making things up please let's go to his office and see for ourselves" he retorted and started leading the way. They all stood up and followed him.

"You cannot violate my privacy," I said running to stand in front of my office door but I was whisked out of the way and they entered my office. I knew I was doomed because Tessy was in there without her skirts on!

Joy my secretary, didn't even know what was going on.

"What do they want sir?"

"Tessy" I replied

"But she's gone" joy said

"Gone?" I could not believe it.

"Yes sir, she left about five minutes ago, she said she had to attend to something very important" I could not believe my luck.

I went back to the boardroom and heaved a big sigh of relief, they were all going to laugh at my dad and believe me completely when I tell them that he is nuts. When they got back my dad was still trying to convince them.

"Honestly I saw her, reliable sources saw her come in and I also heard..."

"Ladies and gentlemen, I suggest we go on with the meeting, daddy is not feeling well right now..."

"You are the one that is not well, look at this boy o" my dad cut in.

"Lets just go ahead and vote" Mrs. Agift said "we don't have all the time in the world"

Mrs. John stood up to conduct the election.

"Those for Dele Martins should please indicate by raising up their right hands"

They all rose up their right hand! Their loyalty to my dad became visible to me.

"It's all settled" Mrs. John said

"Dele Martins is the new head of accounts depar..." my dad was saying when he slumped on the table and passed out. He was rushed to the hospital. Stroke was what he had. I felt guilty somehow, if only I had assured him that Dele was going to get the job… However his behavior that morning really got me surprised, how could he? I realized that my office and whole life was bugged, how else did my dad get all his information or could my secretary be his informant? My mum was shattered but as usual she kept her head up, we kept everything from Yvonne because we didn't want to disturb her studies. Happy finally came to see my dad. I guess that's what brought him round. She transferred him to their hospital in Abuja for proper medical care. My secretary cried when I accused her of being a spy, she could not believe my lack of trust. I checked everywhere but saw no bugs. I would have reported to the police that my life and Tessy's were threatened because I had a strong conviction that they were trailing us everywhere but my mum objected. Tessy's joblessness didn't last long anyway she applied to a pharmaceutical company and was invited for interview. I was supposed to pick her up from the interview but it skipped my memory because I had an August visitor. Kate finally came back to town from London! Seeing her was a pleasant surprise. We were so engrossed in each other that I forgot my appointment with Tessy. Kate had gone for six years! You know the feeling you get when someone who went away for six years just appears. I took her for lunch where we talked and talked.

Kate didn't leave till I closed because she had to do something on the Internet. We left the office at about seven p.m. I saw her off to her car and we talked a while, I asked her when she was leaving,

"Actually I came because of the wedding and Intend to leave immediately after the wedding. Except of course I find something or someone that could keep me here" she said smiling

"The wedding?" I inquired, "who is getting married?'

"Come on Tom, you can't tell me that you know nothing about the wedding!"

Chapter 15

WHEN DELE MARTINS resumed work in the company, I felt so defeated that I avoided him like a plague. My mum advised me to pretend to everybody that I didn't give a damn about him. The guy sure did try all his best to get to me but I guess his best wasn't just good enough. It wasn't easy avoiding two people in the same company. Mac and Dele were people I didn't ever want to set my eyes on. I was still looking for a way of getting Mac out of the company but Dele wasn't my problem, I knew he was going to get out by himself because there were already lots of petitions against him, the guy was misusing the company's fund and all members of the board were pissed off except me. Of course none of them could come to me with complaints because they were the ones that voted for him and not me. My dad recovered from his stroke but he would not come back home claiming he wanted to spend more time with Happy. We knew that he was avoiding mummy and I. I got to the office very early the next morning because I had a lot of work to do; Kate had distracted me the previous day. As I was punching my keyboard, thoughts of Tessy flashed through my mind and I remembered that I had to pick her up from the interview she attended the previous day! I felt so guilty that I could not continue with my work. "Why does Tessy always skip my memory?" I asked myself. I knew that she'd be very angry because there was no justification for my action. I slumped on my table and pictured myself explaining things to Tessy and I knew she was going to....

It took lots of energy but I finished all the urgent work I had to do before I left the office and headed straight for the bottle. I got so drunk that I didn't have problems sleeping. Unfortunately in the middle of the night I woke up feeling terrible.

I blamed my dad and Mac for the way I related with Tessy. I was so attached to them that having a normal relationship with anyone else was becoming impossible. All the anger I thought I had dealt with resurfaced Mac's betrayal, my dads rejection and Dele's victory all brought tears to my eyes and I cried like a little baby. I felt like calling Tessy but what would I say to her? I didn't want to lie to her but that I was so engrossed in another woman and forgot her was not a pleasant thing to say to her. Two days later I fell into an abyss of depression with insomnia as the major symptom. Mummy noticed that I could not sleep at nights so she took me to the hospital to see a doctor.

"Tom Dr Kolade is an expert; I assure you that you will get better immediately you see him"

"Alright mum, if you say so"

I went to see Dr. kolade who asked me a lot of questions and finally diagnosed. He was a very interesting person and was doing his job simply because he loved it.

"Sir, I must confess that no doctor has shown me such enormous concern in my life. I feel better already"

"This statement goes further to reveal that my diagnosis is correct, you have an affective disorder. You feel better now but you are not actually better"

"Affective disorder?"

"Yes, you see in med school I read about Osler and his philoso-phy was 'listen to the patient he is telling you the diagnosis' that's why I had to ask you a lot of questions"

"I see"

"Tom you are depressed. However different types of depression exist but I can't classify yours right now"

"Really?"

"Yes…"

We talked much more and I told him everything about myself. He felt so sorry for me and advised me to make up with my dad and Mac. He also talked to me about real love.

"Tom, I don't think that you are seriously in love with this lady"

"Hey doc, you are sounding just like her"

"Sorry to bust your bubble but that is exactly what it seems" I looked at him blandly.

"Tom, love is an emotion that is like smoke you can't hide it"

"It's not as if I'm hiding my feelings for her…"

"Then the feelings don't exist"

"It does exist, It's just that I have a lot on my mind right now"

"My son, let go of the past experiences you had with women and start all over again. You have this feeling that women are no good so you don't commit yourself to them"

"You are right. I had some nasty experiences but Tessy is not like any of those girls she is so decent. Do you know that it took me five years to ask her out and she was surprised when I did? I love her so much because she allows me be a man"

"You mean other girls make you feel lesser than a man?"

"Yes, some women ask me out and that really pisses me off because they are trying to silently tell me that they are men while I am a woman"

"Hey that's not right"

"I don't know why but I think I can never live without Tessy because she is as proud as a peacock"

"Tom you are so funny"

"I'm very serious doc, there were ladies I was close to in the past just like Tessy but they stupidly fell in love with me even though I did not ask them out, some even went as far as asking me out"

"I can see you have a problem with women expressing the way they feel about a man but, you are wrong you know, as I said earlier love is like smoke you can't hide it. Probably Tessy does not love you"

"I know she does"

"Then why was she surprised when you asked her out?"

"She was pretending to be surprised, just the way a perfect woman should"

"Hmm" Dr. Kolade sighed. "Tom, you and this girl of yours are just pretending to each other it seems you believe that love is a game"

"Not at all, I believe in love"

"I am convinced you have made up your mind about this girl. You love her for your own reasons but she might just dump you one day because I don't think that she feels so deeply about you. Women are all the same they can't hide their emotions they always lose control"

"My Tessy is a rare gem, she is so different from other women, and it's a man's world doc, I choose who should love me"

"You are just a male chauvinist I do not believe that a woman must pretend to a man to be a real woman. Love is all about respect, understanding, trust and passion"

"Passion?"

"Yes Tom, I am talking from experience. A woman you can live with all the days of your life is someone you see and your blood gets hot"

"Hey doc, that is lust"

"Seems that way but it's just what keeps a marriage"

"I beg to disagree"

"You are young so please don't make the mistake that some of us made, after five years of marriage I discovered my sparks and that changed my life"

"How?"

"I just could not ignore the woman that made my blood boil so vigorously"

"Wow"

"So I drifted into an extramarital affair and I nearly ended up marrying another wife"

"What stopped you?"

"The fear of the unknown…she was also married so it was very complicated…but the relationship spanned for about twenty years"

"Quite a long time"

"Yes, and those were the happiest days of my life…I love her so much…don't let me bore you…?

"You are not boring me, the issue of cheating on your wife is something you decide to do or not to do, it can't just happen. I will never cheat on my wife"

"Hmm laudable my son, I also did not plan for such a life, but she just came into my life and that was it…don't judge me boy!"

Our discussion did come to an end after a lot of argument. He was of the opinion that my relationship with Tessy was not real. I learnt something anyway, he thought me how to show love to a woman. After a while Tessy came to see me. I could not believe that she would come; it was then I realized that she loved me so much.

"Are you not going to at least congratulate me? I got the job"

"Congratulations" I said

"Tom, I see no reason why you cannot call to tell me that you're no longer interested, at least courtesy demands that you end the relationship in a civilized manner and not just run off like that"

I kept staring down at my table and could still not utter a word.

"Why have you decided to make my life miserable? I regret ever meeting you Tom and I hate…"

She was already in tears and was about to run out of my office when I rushed to her and hugged her tightly, caressing her hair.

"Tessy, there's no justification for my action. I know that but I swear by my God, I haven't been myself lately. I know I should have called but I was in a very bad mood. I had a misunderstanding with my dad and I got really depressed…"

"That's what you keep saying, the other day you made me prepare dinner and you never showed up claiming you were depressed"

"Tessy this depression was more terrible I was not just blue but dark blue…"

"You are exaggerating"

"We have to go and see the doctor that helped me so that he will explain everything to you"

"Tom, what was the essence of our relationship to be together in only good times? I wanted to be part of your life completely in good times and bad times, to share all your ups and downs and for you to also share mine"

"Tessy why the use of 'was' that 'was' was supposed to be an 'is' Tessy please you cannot just walk out of my life because of this one mistake, I am just recovering from depression. I am so fragile please Tess don't get me depressed again. From now henceforth you are a part of me, in good times and bad times"

"You are sure you'll never repeat this?" she asked,

"Of course" I replied, "cross my heart"

"O.k., I'll take you on your word but only after I see your doctor, I want to find out more about this depression you had"

"Thank you very much," I said lifting her up and hugging her tightly.

"You owe me something Tess"

"What?" she inquired,

"The kiss you promised"

"Oh that"

"Don't tell me that you are still scared of kissing me because…." She shut my mouth up with her own and kissed me passionately in a way that no one had ever done before.

"Tessy let's go and celebrate your new job" I said when we finally caught our breaths. I went home after a really nice time with Tessy to find Yvonne in the house. She was through with nursing school and was I not proud of her?

But she was not very happy; she confessed that her exams were difficult

"The result is coming out in two months and I might spend an extra year if I fail"

"Come on Yvonne you are already a nurse, I see your scripts" I said shutting my eyes tightly as if I was receiving revelation, "wow look at those A's"

She smiled broadly but I could see tears in her eyes,

"What's wrong Yvonne?"

"Nothing I just feel somehow graduating from school, did you feel the same way?"

"Yes I did," I said, recalling the day I graduated.

When I got to my room I called the doctor and told him to help me convince Tessy to go soft with me and he agreed. I was very happy that night. I decided that there was no point procrastinating, I loved Tessy and wanted to spend the rest of my life with her. I made up my mind to propose to her. I was going to marry Tessy! But the thought of marriage made me feel so cold down to my spines...

As I was about to start sleeping there was a knock at my door.

"Come in" I said feeling irritated. It was Yvonne

"Yvonne what's up?" I inquired

"Why didn't you tell me about the wedding?"

"What wedding?"

"Come on Tom, you know the wedding I'm talking about"

Chapter 16

WE ALL PLANNED for the wedding even though it was short notice but why it bothered me so much was because everyone believed that I knew about the wedding, while I was the last person to find out about the wedding. No one could believe it, even I myself could not believe it but it was actually happening, the wedding was taking place in exactly ten days. The news was the hottest in town. Everyone marveled at the lucky bride who was anonymous, as no one had met her before. It was annoying that no one believed that the wedding would ever take place because they had this feeling that the groom was going to change his mind or run away because he was already labeled a bachelor for life. The reason why I could not believe it was that I had not seen Mac with any girl, it was as if she cast a spell on him. Mac jumping into something that was for a lifetime in such a manner was beyond me.

Yvonne broke down again; she was so stupid. She could not just accept the fact that her relationship with Mac was finally over because she had this strong conviction that they were meant to be till eternity.

In as much as I hated what she was doing, I could not neglect her. I stood firmly by her encouraging her.

Kate came to the house once more to plead with me to make up with Mac, she could not understand what went wrong between us and I was not in any position to reveal Yvonne's secret.

"Yvonne you have to relocate for some time" Kate said

"Relocate where?" Yvonne and I inquired

"To our house, there's so much to be done in so short a time, we need all the help we can get. As for you Tom" she continued, "this is a perfect time for you to make up with Mac, he needs you so much, the least you could do is to be there for him" I had nothing to say. Yvonne told Kate she'd be there the next day, after Kate left I talked Yvonne out of going to their house. When it was three days to the wedding Mac called me at the Office. I was surprised considering the fact that I knew the kind of ego he had. I was sure that it took him more than enough courage because his pride was more than that of a Peacock and I was ready to make him feel bad.

"Hi Tom"

"Hello Mac" I replied

"Em, actually Tom I was thinking... You see I searched all round the world for a best man but I could find none, please would you mind being my best man?"

"You want me to be your best man?"

"Yes Tom, I want that more than I've ever wanted anything in my life"

"But Mac, you can't be serious"

"Of course Tom, I'm dead serious I want you to be my best man"

"Mac I am flattered I must confess but I'm sorry, I can't be your best man. I would have loved to but, it's your fault anyway, I mean the best man doesn't get informed that he's best man three days before a wedding" I could feel his ego getting deflated like a punctured tire and how happy I felt.

"Come on Tom, don't play hard with me remember how far we've come, lets cross this hurdle Tom, lets put this quarrel behind us for God's sake please, don't make me beg you...."

"Mac, this hurdle is rather too high I won't be able to cross it right now, I'll have to really practice hard and look Mac you've not searched hard enough, I mean you've only searched the world, how about searching out of space, you know, like other planets, I suggest mars!"

Then I hung up on him. At first I felt very happy turning Mac down, later the offer kept tempting me but I stood my grounds. My heart became more hardened when I saw how broken my little sister was.

How could Mac want me to be his best man after dumping my sister and breaking her heart into tiny bits?

I had to personally go and shop for something very beautiful for Yvonne to wear for the wedding. I wanted the best money could buy; she had to be the best-dressed girl at the wedding, even better than the bride herself. Yvonne looked simply ravishing when she tried it on that her spirits became lifted immediately. I had no idea that she had such beautiful curves.

The 'D' day finally came and we all went to church for the service. Tessy traveled home to see her sick aunt, which left me with just Yvonne. I had to hold Yvonne's hand as we sat down.

"Oh Tom, I have to leave, I can't stand seeing Mac get married" she whispered into my ear.

Mac was already at the altar and his bride was about to march in.

"Tom please let's leave, I'll fight her if I ever set my eyes on her, please let's leave or I'll die"

"No Yvonne, you'll stay right here and you won't die. Behave yourself. Please don't make a fool out of us..." she simply nodded.

"Now there it is on the floor" I pointed to the floor, Yvonne was confused.

"What's on the floor?" she inquired seeing nothing as she looked down.

"It's the smile that you dropped, now come on pick it up and wear it". Yvonne started smiling

"That's my girl," I said pressing her hand tightly. The bride marched in and the pastor began the ceremony.

"…Is there anyone here who has any objection as to the joining of these people, please step forth or forever hold your peace?" Someone walked in angrily and shouted

"Yes there is" Everyone was surprised.

"Why?" inquired the pastor

"She is my fiancée" he answered, "Linda", he continued, "How could you throw away eight years in this way"

"Tom this cannot be happening" Yvonne said

"Look Emeka" Linda replied, "for eight years you've not started any wedding plans, you have not even proposed to me and you stand there calling me your fiancée?"

"You know I'm waiting for the right time," replied Emeka.

"Right time?" asked Linda, "when would the right time be?"

"Linda, I love you and I know that you love me too"

"I am sorry" Mac cut in, "she is no longer in love with you but me"

"Shut up" Linda yelled at Mac, "Stay out of this"

"What do you mean," Mac yelled back, "how can I stay out of something that affects my own wedding?"

"Linda, I planned to finish building the house at the village before I finally settle down, besides you can't blame me, you always gave me the impression that you were not in a hurry to get married. But Linda, if you can end this marriage right now, I swear by my God that we'll get married anytime you want" Emeka pleaded and Linda turned to Mac.

"I'm very sorry, I can't go ahead with this marriage we hardly know each other, Emeka is the love of my life" then she turned to Emeka,

"Please forgive me"

"No problem sweetheart, I should be the one asking for forgiveness, I pushed you into this"

She ran into his waiting arms, embraced him and they walked out of the church together. That was the end of Mac's wedding. Everywhere was in utter chaos. The two families apologized to their invited to guests. Mac was completely thrown of balance and devastated that he could not move, believe me there's no sorrow as heavy as being jilted at the altar. Yvonne started humming to herself

"Jesus loves me now I know…"

"Shut up Yvonne we are not supposed to marvel in public, let's go and say sorry to Mac"

We walked up to Mac

"I'm sorry Mac" said Yvonne, "but the way she jilted you is more pathetic than the way you jilted me…"

"Mac", I cut in, "Em, it's so funny I just feel like laughing, I'm simply glad I'm not your best man"

Chapter 17

MAC'S WEDDING FIASCO was talk of the town, his whole family were humiliated especially his best man Tony. Mr. Mac was obviously not bothered.

Yvonne was too happy for my liking I hoped that she was happy simply because of Mac's misfortune and not due to the fact that he was still single.

I ran into Mac at the office one morning and tried to spite him.

"Good morning Mac" I said, Mac could not believe it; he turned and stared at me.

"I'm sorry I've still not gotten you a condolence card,"

"A condolence card? What for?" inquired Mac

"For your em, dead heart or heartbreak of course, which ever"

"Oh thanks" Mac replied, but no thanks because my heart isn't broken or dead as you think, I was disappointed yes, but heart-broken? I don't think so"

"I'm glad to hear that" I replied and walked away.

There was no wedding any more but Kate Donald refused to go back to London. We were still close like old times and I had no second thoughts when she kept visiting me daily, even at odd hours.

One afternoon Kate came and hurried me into her car for an impromptu lunch date. It was fun anyway as no one had ever whisked me away in that manner, and it was really romantic. She took me somewhere I had never gone before. We ate, and talked on end. Before I knew what was happening it was already a few minutes before six p.m. oh! How time flies when you're having fun.

I marched into the office to grab my suitcase and head for home to behold Tessy on my computer. Damn me, I forgot our lunch date! I nearly ran out of the office but I was too late, she'd already seen me.

"How was your day? Don't just stand there staring at me," she said

"So, so" I replied "and yours"

"Hmm mine was terrible, I nearly starved to death. I waited and waited and wait..."

"Oh Tessy I'm so sorry, I forgot..."

"That's just what I wanted to hear, you forgot, you always forget when it comes to me Tom, you always forget"

"Come on Tess, that's not a fair thing to say".

"Ohhh, so it's a fair thing to say to me, its fair that you always forget our dates, I called in the afternoon and was told that you went out for an urgent meeting, then I called two more times and the reply was 'he's not back' I came immediately after work and decided to wait because I saw your car. I can see how urgent..."

"Tessy I have nothing to say for myself, but, honestly it was not intentional, I swear God knows that I didn't do it intentionally".

"Tom, I'm not saying you did it intentionally all I'm saying is that I am not an important figure in your life. You always forget when it comes to me, Tom I am not in your heart, and you are not in love with me"

"No Tessy don't say that, for God's sake please hear me out, remember what the doctor said to you about how fragile I am? Please don't make me depressed. I love you, sincerely the very first day I set my eyes on you I knew you were going to be mine, I fell in love with you even before you moved into the apartment, believe me Tessy, the day I saw you at my doorstep I could not believe it. It was like a dream come true. Tessy I love you and nothing can change that."

"Not even the lady that brought you back a few minutes ago, a lady you spent the whole day doing whatever with?"

"Yes Tessy not even her can change the love I have for you...." She started weeping,

"No Tom, you are found of me what kind of love is this, the kind of love you profess is different from the type of love I want. Tom I can't have you messing up my life. It's no use Tom, this relationship is not real. All you love is yourself and family especially yourself. You are a self-centered bigot"

She ran out of my office, and I raced after her but before I could catch up with her she jumped on a bike, which sped off. A self-centered bigot was what I really was. I felt ashamed of myself. I myself could not believe that my girlfriend still hopped on bikes.

I went back to the office, got my things and headed straight for her house, I knocked and knocked and knocked but she would not open the door, I went home dejected that night.

My childhood could not just let me go. People I was really close to during my childhood were still the closest people to me. I realized that it would take special efforts on my part to include Tessy in my circle of friends. I had to get Tessy back by hook or by crook just anyhow. First thing the next morning I went to her place. She would still not see me so I dropped a note pleading with her to reconsider. In the afternoon I sent her Lunch from her favorite restaurant and a note pleading with her to reply but there was no reply. I went to her house that evening but she would still not see me.

A week later, I bought a car for Tessy, a cute little car; I thought it was going to blow her mind away but Tessy would still not see me, she didn't even send a thank you for the car which she accepted with great happiness.

I had never chased a woman the way I was chasing after Tessy; every thirty minutes, I would call her and she would hang up immediately she hears my voice. It was an interesting experience anyway. "I must conquer," I kept telling myself.

Finally I decided to try for the last time, I went to her house knocked but she would not open the door as usual.

"Tessy, I know you're listening, I'm going to stand right here until you come out"

At about ten p.m. I almost gave up, how could she keep me outside for five hours. I decided to stay there till morning so I called home and told them. Ten p.m became eleven p.m. By twelve p.m. Tessy went to bed as I saw the lights in her sitting room go off.

"Goodnight Tessy, I screamed, "I hope you'll dream about me." I entered my car and started sleeping too. At about two a.m there was a tap on my shoulder. Tessy was standing a centimeter away from me!

"Why don't you come in so that you could sleep more comfortably?"

"Emmm... I'm very grateful" I replied. I jumped out of the car and followed her before she would change her mind. As we got in, she locked the door behind her. I walked to the sofa and slumped on it.

"Come right in" she said. Right into where? I thought was I not already in?

"You want to sleep on the sofa?" she asked surprised. Was she expecting me to sleep on the floor? I asked myself.

"Come right in Tom, my bed is big enough for two..."

Chapter 18

HEY, DON'T THINK what you are thinking because nothing happened that night. It would have been better if I slept on the sofa jeje.

To say the truth I thought that something was going to happen you know a kind of reconciliation on the bed but my Tessy slept at one end of the bed and told me a stern good night before she wrapped herself up completely with her blanket, when I say completely I mean with her head and toes. The blanket was white so she looked exactly like a mummy. The sight was so horrible that I had to lie down at the other end and face the other side to prevent nightmares. Two a.m became three a.m and I could find no sleep, all I could do was to think of my next line of action. Did she expect me to sleep like that or did she expect me to do something? I decided to be a man and do something. But what if she was not expecting me to do anything? My attempting to do something might jeopardize my chances, which looked very slim... somehow the angel of sleep overtook me and I slept. The next morning Tessy woke me up.

"It's time for breakfast" she said and disappeared, there was no good morning. I washed my face and went into the dining area to behold the table!

"Tessy"

"shsh just sit down" she whispered and I sat down

"Now, all this is for the most romantic guy on earth, Tom I never knew that you could be so romantic, sleeping in the car, and every other thing you've done..." she opened the wine,

"I am going to make a toast now, here is your glass. To the most romantic guy on earth, may you remain romantic and to our love, may it continue to grow until eternity"

That day was the most memorable day of my life; I had no idea, that Tessy could be so romantic.

We didn't go to work throughout the day we both called our respective offices and lied.

We talked at length. It was on that day that Tessy let me into her life completely, she told me about her family. The woman she calls mummy was actually her auntie who brought her up from age four after her parents died in a ghastly motor accident. Her mum was six months pregnant when she died leaving Tessy an only child. Her auntie made sure that she got her education.

In a nutshell Tessy's childhood was traumatic, never did she experience parental love, she confessed to me that she was starved of love.

"Tom all I need is someone who would love me as a mother, care for me as a father and be there for me as a sibling, I guess that will not be an easy task for just one person"

"Tess, I promise to be that person you've been searching for, now that I know, the whole thing will be much easier"

"Tom having been deprived of love for a long time my demands are sort of too much, a lot of guys say I complain a lot and all that."

"No Tess I guess it's because they've never known the underlying cause of your sensitivity, Tessy I understand perfectly and I swear not to let you down."

"Are you sure Tom? Rejection and neglect breaks me apart, are you sure you can do all you're promising?"

"Yes Tessy I am sure, I know I won't let you down because of the love I have for you, never have I loved like this and I'm sure that we are destined for each other"

"I think so too" she replied. "We are destined to be together until eternity"

Chapter 19

YVONNE'S RESULT FINALLY came out and she made it, everyone was very happy for her, I especially because I knew what she went through at that period of her break up with Mac. I was also very happy because she was herself again, no more weeping because of Mac; she had completely come round.

My mum organized a party for Yvonne to commemorate all her successes; becoming a nurse and adding another year. Happy and her family were coming with my dad to attend our little sister's dinner party. It was indeed going to be a big party and I was already counting down to it. Trust me; I selected the best outfit for Yvonne and Tessy. Yvonne's was a Lilac evening gown with spaghetti straps, while Tessy's was silver with no sleeves at all.

A lot of people came for the party; I introduced Kate to Tessy as the lady I went out with that afternoon and I introduced Tessy to Kate as my sweet heart. Kate's countenance changed a bit but she quickly gathered herself together. I noticed that Kate did not approve of Tessy for a reason I could not fathom

"I love your gown Tessy, are you a fashion designer?" asked Kate

"No I'm not" Tessy replied, "Tom is the fashion designer"

"Wow! Exclaimed Tessy, "Tommy, I had no idea that you are a fashion designer"

"I am not really a fashion designer" I replied "I'm just good at choosing already designed clothes"

We all laughed at that. I wanted Tessy and Kate to get to know each other so I excused myself.

"Ladies, I have to fix something right now I'll be back in a few minutes so grab the opportunity and get to know each other"

"Alright" they chorused both smiling at me. When I came back, Tessy and Kate stopped talking.

"Wow, Tom this girl is brilliant, why have you been hiding her away from me?" Kate asked. I felt flattered, but funny enough Tessy didn't smile.

"Come Tom, let's dance, you have to tell me everything about Tessy..."

Before I could object she led me to the dance floor, the next minute I turned around and Tessy was no longer where we left her. I scanned the whole room for her but I didn't catch a glimpse of her. Immediately after the dance, I went in search of Tessy. I searched the entire house inside and out, and finally went to the guards and asked if they saw anyone with Tessy's description leaving.

"Oga, we see her Ip to say you see the sfeed wey she carry wallahi tallahi bilahilazi you go pear"

I walked back at a loss of what to do, and then I became angry, what went wrong? I recalled my conversation with Kate while she was with us and didn't discover any flaws on my part. I sat down outside and wondered why Tessy behaved this way. No way, nothing on earth was going to make me go through all that pleading again I concluded.

Then I recalled that she left speeding, how could an armature driver speed like that in the night? What if she has an accident? I decided to call her house, immediately she picked the phone I hung up, knowing she arrived home safely calmed me down. When I heard everyone clapping, I stood up and went inside,

Yvonne was about to make her speech and cut her lovely cake courtesy of happy, and then I saw MAC! What was the son of a bitch doing here? I knew that Yvonne didn't invite him so I decided to walk up to him immediately after the speech and ask him to leave. I hoped that Yvonne would not see him. Damn him for coming on a very important day in Yvonne's life like this, his coming would rekindle old memories in Yvonne, which could ruin her great day.

"Today is a very joyous day for me. I am actually celebrating three very important things in my life, which I consider the most important aspects of my life..."

"Three things?" I asked myself because I only knew about two.

"The first is my birthday; today I am a year older"

We all sang a birthday song for her.

"The second is that I am now qualified to give injections, so any of you that falls sick should come for injections..." Everyone laughed and clapped for her

"It would not be free..."

"Ohhh" they all chorused

"But it won't be expensive either" they clapped for her

Last but not the least is my wedding" That got everybody crazy, even I myself could not believe it, wedding to whom?

"Today I make it public that I and Macilinus Donald have been engaged and are going to get married in a month!"

Everyone gave her a standing ovation. My mum and Mac's mum were the happiest; they rushed and embraced each other.

"I am now going to call on my husband- to_be to participate in the cutting of this cake,"

Mac walked up to her and they both cut the cake, after cutting the cake, they hugged each other...

It was terrible for me; shock waves ran down my spines. No, Yvonne could not do this, what got into her? Yvonne and Mac right behind my back again? I simply could not take it.

I excused Yvonne and dragged her to the kitchen

"Tom, you're hurting me, what have I done to..."

"What have you done? Yvonne please what's this nonsense with Mac"

"Tom I'm sorry I didn't tell you, I just didn't know how to break the news to you"

"After all he did to you, after all your sleepless nights, after your suicidal attempt you still went back to that pig"

"Mac is not a pig"

"Wow, this is getting more interesting Yvonne you are completely insane because I can remember vividly the day you named him a pig"

"Yes Tom, I said a lot of terrible things about Mac out of anger, I'll appreciate it if you never refer to them in the future"

"Tell me Yvonne, what if Mac had gotten married, would you have truly committed suicide? Sorry that's a silly question; of course you would have hung yourself. What he did to you was debauching, he made you less than a human being. Jesus Christ Yvonne you are..."

"I am a person with a good heart, what's so unholy in making up with someone? Please don't ruin my day Tom please"

"You are getting me wrong, there's nothing wrong with making up with him, but going out with him all over again is simply wrong not to talk of marrying him... After all I went through because of you, the least you could do is to show a little consideration..."

"Look here and listen carefully Tom, I really can't remember asking you to assist me in anyway, your fight with Mac was totally your business and not mine and let me tell you about a lesson I learnt from the bible, God's experience with Adam revealed that whenever you do something that is not asked of you, disaster occurs. Adam never asked God for a helpmate he never told God that he was lonely; he didn't even know the meaning of loneliness! God created Eve on his own free will and caused the downfall of man"

"Bravo, Yvonne that was an excellent speech"

"Thank you Tom and em...If you don't mind I'm going back to my guests before they start searching for me"

"I do mind Yvonne, so this is all I get for what I went through because of you, from your speech all I could gather is that I am a busybody"

"If you say so," she said opening the kitchen door. I rushed after her, grabbed her arm, turned her around, gave her a slap and walked out of the kitchen. I went straight to my room, grabbed my car keys and drove out. There was nowhere I could go to except to a bar as Tessy's place was out of the question. Yvonne was right; I wasn't supposed to involve myself. I went somewhere nice and got drunk. I had to sleep a while in the car before I could drive home, and when I got home it was two a.m. I tiptoed into my room, took off my clothes and went to bed then I realized that someone was on my bed, who could it be? It was Mac, he stood up and walked up to me, I could not utter a word we ran into each other's arms and started laughing hysterically of course that night, sleep was banished as we talked till morning.

Chapter 20

MAC AND YVONNE finally got married I was the best man of course. They moved into Mac's very beautiful house, which I went to see before the wedding.

"Come on Mac, this house is too big"

"Don't worry, it will soon be too small because we intend to fill everywhere up with children"

"No Mac, you won't turn my sister into a baby producing factory" We both laughed at that. I was so envious of Mac that I started thinking about getting married without feeling cold to my spines. Tessy apologized for leaving Yvonne's party claiming she had a severe attack of jealousy. I accepted her apology and after three weeks I proposed to her. She gladly accepted so our wedding preparations started immediately. My Mum adored Tessy but I never got to know my dad's impression, as his attitude problem had still not vanished even after his long stay with happy receiving the best form of treatment.

Travelling down to Tessy's village for the introduction and traditional Marriage was a refreshing adventure for me; it was the
first time in my life that I would visit a place so remote.

Tessy fell in love with me a hundred times over when I didn't
complain but adapted immediately. We stayed there for a week instead of three days and I was still not ready to leave, her auntie also
could not help but love me. After pleas from Tessy and her uncles,
I finally accepted to leave. It wasn't as if I enjoyed every bit of my
stay, but I did all I did because the way to a woman's heart is by
doing extraordinary things. I came back finally but my life became
hell. Kate would not let me breathe. She was around me every day
and everywhere. Tessy was so unhappy about the way I was carry-
ing on with Kate but there was nothing I could do about it without
hurting Kate's feelings, and I didn't want to. It tore me apart that I
had to hurt Kate to safeguard my relationship with Tessy.

One fateful day, Kate came to take me out for lunch but I declined politely that I was taking my fiancée out for lunch as well.

"Nonsense" she said, "we could all go for lunch together..."

What was I supposed to say to that? We drove to Tessy's office
to pick her up but she said she wasn't going anymore when I told
her that Kate was outside and wanted to join us.

"Why the change of mind?" I inquired

"Why the presence of Kate?" She replied.

"I don't know why you should keep nagging over Kate, she's
like a sister"

"A sister? Come on Tom, even a blind man would see that the
girl is after you"

"After me? She cannot be. You are simply jealous, jealous of
someone as harmless as Kate"

"Harmless? Tom I have a confession to make I honestly didn't
want to tell you but I guess keeping it will not help matters, Tom
from that night of Yvonne's party Kate has been asking me to
break up with you. She offered me money on several occasions"

"Shut up Tessy, you are making this up, Kate would never do
such a thing, how dare you" I was really pissed off; Tessy's sense
of insecurity was beyond me.

"Yes Tom, I know you will not believe me but it's true, she's been telling me a lot of things about you and...." I had heard enough. I walked out on her.

"What took you so long?" Kate inquired

"She was busy so I had to wait, let's go Kate, she's not coming with us."

"Why?" she inquired sadly

"She's busy"

"Oh oh, then we'll have to eat lunch without her" she said and drove to the restaurant. As we sat down to eat lunch, she noticed I was moody. She continued chatting but I didn't respond the usual way.

"What's wrong with you Tom?" she inquired, "this is quite unlike you"

"Quite unlike me right? Actually Kate there's something wrong, it's something that has to do with you"

"Me?"

"Yes Kate, and I want an honest answer right here and now"

"Out with it Tom"

"What do you want from me?"

"I beg your pardon"

"You heard me right Kate, why have you been offering Tessy money to leave me?"

"Honestly Tom, I don't know what you're talking about, offer Tessy money? Whatever for?"

"That's what I want you to tell me" I replied.

"I don't know what you're talking about, why would Tessy do this to me?"

"Then tell me Kate, why have you been pestering me, why the sudden lunch and dinner invitations, why the sudden attention?"

"Oh my God, Tom you misunderstand everything, I pay attention to you because we've been friends from childhood and you are like a brother to me, I can't believe that you would ever make such accusations. I am disappointed in you_.. I guess I'd better leave"

She fled before I could utter another word. Who was saying the truth, was it Tessy or Kate. I sat down there for an hour thinking. Why would Tessy make up a story like that knowing fully well what the implications could be, if she framed Kate up because of her stupid sense of insecurity and inferiority complex it would be over between us. Could Kate on the other hand be that crafty? Was I blowing her attention on me out of proportion? Was it possible that Kate loved me and saw Tessy as an obstacle? I could not answer any of these questions.

I took a taxi back to the office to meet some files on my table; they were the Kanuri Project Files. I went through it and discovered that the figures were outrageous. Nothing could ever make me sign something like that! I summoned Dele martins for the first time, in spite of my disdain for him; I had to see him just this once to tell him exactly what I thought of him.

My defense mechanism had been to ignore him. I knew he spent sleepless nights plotting how to get to me because I also spent sleepless nights plotting how to avoid him, which I've been doing perfectly well until now. My foul mood and pent up anger needed to be unleashed on someone and I chose Dele Martins.

He appeared immediately in his immaculately tailored suit. His perfume filled my whole office despite the air conditioner that was on. He smelt and looked money, and it was obvious how he made his money.

"What are these?" I asked pointing at the Kanuri Project files on my table

"This is the Kanuri Project files, the heading is bold enough"

"Yes I know it's the Kanuri project but what I don't understand are the figures. How could you bring a proposal of fifty million and expect me to sign?"

"Now you are talking" said Dele, "your problem is that the figures appear outrageous"

"Thank God you are understanding, Yes Mr Martins, the figures are outrageous, I went through the bids last week, and I saw bids of twenty million, twenty five and thirty..."

"What I want is excellence at whatever cost"

"I also want excellence but at a reasonable price" I said "POMO Constructions have handled lots of jobs for us in the past and they are very good, their bid is twenty-five million and I suggest that we go for it"

"Someone recommended MUNA Constructions there's no harm trying new grounds"

"Really? I asked, "There's no harm? Even when it's obvious that their figures seem outrageous?"

"Mr. Davies, the company has the money fifty million is not something that can ever make the company go under."

"Mr. Dele martins, little drops of water make the mighty ocean, now get your silly papers and get out of my office I'm not signing"

"I'll send my secretary to get them," he said and walked out of my office majestically.

"At least, I sent him out of my office" I told myself happily, I was about to call Mac and tell him what transpired between Dele and I when he rushed into my office

"Tom, something very terrible has happened"

Chapter 21

KATE'S DEATH WAS a shocker, she ran into a moving truck after she left me. It shook the whole family and I felt very guilty, it was as if I killed her considering what transpired between us and how she left the restaurant. I wished I had not confronted her the way I did, I wished that I allowed things lie just like that, I wished a lot of things but none of my wishes could bring Kate back to life, because wishes can never be horses. Kate left the restaurant so annoyed that she was not driving with care, I killed Kate was all I could tell myself. I remembered what Mrs. Donald once said to me about the key of Kate's life and death lying in my hands...

Yvonne cried the most. Mr. and Mrs. Donald were expressionless, they had been expecting her death all their lives but not through a car accident anyway. Tears could not form in my eyes but my heart was all tears and anguish. No one knew that I was the last person Kate saw on earth.

At Kate's burial I saw Tessy, we were gazing at each other, I had to transfer this guilt I was feeling to Tessy because she was actually responsible. Tessy was in tears, she ran into my arms so I had no option but to embrace her. I felt that everyone was looking at us because we were the culprits that sent Kate to her death. We entered the car and talked.

"Tom I feel so terrible, she died that afternoon I told you about..."

"Yes Tessy" I cut in, "your inferiority complex and gross sense of insecurity made you say horrible things about Kate and damn me for ever thinking twice about what you said..."

"Tom stop this, I didn't lie to you, I told you the truth"

"What truth? Kate denied everything, she was so offended that she left angrily and a few minutes later she died" Tessy brought out a cheque from her bag and gave it to me.

"This is the cheque she gave me that morning, it's a pity that I've destroyed subsequent cheques" This was enough evidence. Exactly Kate's handwriting and signature...I stared at the cheque.

"I can never bring myself to tell you everything that went on between Kate and I. She made my life hell but kept pretending to you" The cheque proved everything to me so Kate had been playing a game all along.

"Tom I feel terrible, its as if I killed her I wish I didn't tell you anything, it was just too much for me to take and oh..." She broke down into fresh sobs. I gathered her into my arms.

"Tessy please forgive me for not believing in you let's put this behind us ok"

Tessy and I got closer from that day. On my wedding day my dad refused to attend claiming paralysis, it didn't bother me, as I had already developed resistance to his attitude problem. Mac's dad stood in for him.

I settled down to family life, and discovered that it was totally a whole new ball game, moving out of the house made my mum very sad because of loneliness.

I felt pity for her, all her children were gone leaving her with a husband that kept avoiding her. At first I made it a point of duty to visit her every day after a month it became less frequently until it completely stopped because I just could not find the time.

When my wife got pregnant, things got more hectic for me. I didn't want anything to happen to my unborn baby so my wife had to be properly taken care of. I made sure that I was always there for her and also ensured that she lacked nothing, she even complained that I was fussing over her too much but I couldn't help it as thoughts of becoming a father got me excited.

When Mac's twins were born, my anxiety increased, every evening I would drive to Mac's house after work to see the babies until mine finally came. I named her Elizabeth_ the Queen of my heart. There were three new babies in the Davies family and I loved them so much. I swore to love my children all my life and never shut them out of my life the way my dad did to me. My dad never visited me but kept going to visit Yvonne and the twins, that didn't bother me. My mum moved into my house to help me with the baby as Tessy had to go back to work, everyone was like why should mummy neglect a sick husband not knowing that he didn't want her around. To avoid wagging tongues, her stay with me had to be cut short and we employed the services of a maid.

Everyone laughed at us when Tessy, got pregnant again, this time it was not easy at all, Tessy kept nagging, perhaps she was thinking of the pain she went through just a year ago, Elizabeth tore her apart so badly that she could not sit down for some time because of the stitches.

Anyway Tessy, the mother of my daughter grew more beautiful each day in my eyes, the love I had for her overwhelmed me and it got stronger with every passing day. I would be in the office daydreaming about Tessy and Elizabeth.

But what pained me was that Tessy's love for me became colder, she didn't care about me the way she used to, a kind of reversal of roles occurred. I didn't know how to handle such neglects, at a point I started complaining that she was giving Elizabeth and the pregnancy more attention than me, her reply was that I am suffering from a kind of poetic justice, Whatever that meant I had no idea.

"Tom I know that right now I'm ugly, "I won't blame you if you start seeing someone else"

"Tessy, for once believe that you are beautiful, do something about this insecurity problem of yours else I'll go crazy"

"Yes tom go crazy, you can't suddenly start showering me with love and attention when I'm all round and ugly"

"You are not round or ugly to me, I am serious you are so cute"

"I don't believe you, this excessive display of affection is like a pretext..."

I shut her mouth up with a kiss, carried her to the bedroom and reassured her as much as I could but at the end of the day she remained down cast. Her mood swings were beyond me.

I blamed Tessy's behaviour on her childhood, which was very traumatic. All my misunderstandings with Tessy boiled down to feelings of insecurity. Even in marriage she still had the feeling that one day the marriage would come crashing on her. She had no faith in anything. I was trying all my best to make her feel secure only to get more and more accusations. Her most used sentence was "Tom you don't love me", "stop pretending" or "Tom if you really loved me you would have done this or that.

I prayed to God for a son and He answered. I named my son David for I knew that he would be a man after God's own heart.

"Was that the end of life?" I asked myself, what was left for me? I had a good job and a cute family. I felt I had achieved everything in life or was there more to look forward to? Probably, to have more children and look after them till death. Despite all my sense of fulfillment there was this little vacuum somewhere. It was there so much that I could feel it. I felt that was not the end of life_ like there was much more to my life, more hurdles to cross. I thought of becoming a politician but the thought only put a smile on my face. As I sat down there thinking of my next line of action, I heard Tessy scream out my name

"Tom where the hell are you?"

"Sweetheart I'm here" I called out

"Where is here" she said

"At the balcony" I replied

She rushed to the balcony

"Oh Tom, two things have happened"

"Two things?"

"Something good and something bad which do you want to hear first"

"What is the something good?"

"Yvonne has given birth to twins again"

"What?" The news was simply incredible.

"Yes Tom, two girls this time"

"Then what's the bad news?" I asked

"Tom, it's a very sad news, I'm not sure you'll want to hear about it"

"Come on Tessy spill it out"

"Oh Tom, I feel so sorry", then she started crying. "Oh Tom your father is dead"

Chapter 22

HOW RIGHT I was the end of life was not just growing up, getting married, having children and dying, I started seeing the hurdles I had to cross to fill that vacuum that was so pronounced in my heart.

Yvonne was pathetic, as our father died on the day she gave birth to her second set of twins. As for my mum, words cannot describe how broken-hearted she was. Happy, her husband and three children flew down immediately. There was sorrow everywhere. It surprised me that despite the fact that everyone knew that he had a terminal ailment, his death still surprised us. Hell, his death shook me. We kept him in the mortuary and commenced his burial arrangements; the house was filled up with people who came to condole the family. We were all surprised when Mr. Alexander came and informed us that the will had to be read before the burial as part of my dad's instructions. We all decided to give in to our dad's wish. The next morning the whole family gathered in the sitting room as Mr. Alexander read the will;

no one was really surprised except for the fact that he left nothing for my mum.

"...I leave all I have to my only son with majority of my shares. To all my grandchildren, I leave them five percent each of my share which dividend would be kept in trust for them until they are eighteen years of age. My daughters have the right to collect any amount of money from my son whenever the need arises. And my son shall give whatever the amount without any question. My son shall be responsible for my burial.

I make my son managing director and my son in law, Macilinus Donald the deputy Managing director. I give the family house to Chioma...."

The lawyer continued reading the will-giving portions to different persons like the driver, stewards and members of our extended. Finally the lawyer concluded.

"Will Mr. Davies son please come and sign here please?"

I stood up dejectedly to go and sign but before I got there, Dele Martins was already there.

"What nonsense?" I asked as the Lawyer handed Dele the papers to sign, every one became confused.

"Mr. Alexander do you think that we are insane?" I inquired. Mac rushed and stopped Dele Martins from signing.

"This is not a place for jokes," Happy said angrily.

"I can explain said Mr. Alexander, actually I should have done that before reading the will but, you see Mr. Davies put me in a very terrible situation of doing this explanation. Tom you are not Mr. Davies' son! I was actually hoping that I would slump and die before revealing this secret. When he discovered that you were not his son, a few months later his son, Dele Martins traced him. He was shocked to the extent of having a heart attack... his first heart attack..."

"Look Mr. Alexander, enough of all these trash" I cut in.

"Actually Tom, it's all such a great coincidence. It all started when you were sick and needed blood transfusion none of your parents could offer you blood"

"Nonsense" mummy replied, "Davies gave Tom blood"

"Yes that's what you people were told but the actual truth is that he bought that blood that was transfused into Tom"

"What!" we all exclaimed. Mr. Alexander continued

"He took Tom's blood and sent it abroad for various tests; the DNA test results revealed that he was not your father"

"Look Mr. Alex" said Mac, "we are going to carry out our own analysis to truly ascertain what you are claiming and if we get contrary results you would be sued to court and you know the implications."

"Yes Mr. Mac Donald, I have everything right here in this files go through it and carry out all necessary verifications."

My dad's body stayed in the mortuary for two months before he was buried because we had to carry out thorough investigations and discovered that Mr. Alex allegations were all true.

We all sat down silently while Dele told us the modalities for my father's burial, which took him a whole week to map out. Everything became crystal clear especially the reason for the hostility my dad displayed to my mum and I. Realizing that I was not his son was a sordid experience. The man I stayed with all my life that gave me all the best that I could ever get out of life was not my father! The coincidence was Dele Martins showing up. Dele Martins his real son tracing him at a point when he discovered that I was not his son was...

On the day of the burial which Dele fixed, we all followed the corpse, Dele and his men were leading the way as no one knew to which cemetery he was taking the corpse. To our greatest surprise, they drove to a riverside. We all got out of our cars,

"What's happening?" Mac asked

"This is not a cemetery," Yvonne added

"Yes" Dele replied, "this is not a cemetery but for now just assume that you are inside a cemetery"

"Why?" Yvonne inquired.

"Zee" he replied and all his men laughed. My dad's coffin was brought down and opened

"Ladies and gentlemen, as my father's son, he bestowed upon me the right or responsibility of seeing to his burial. Dele snapped his fingers and some guys appeared with a gallon of fuel removed my dad from the coffin while Dele gave a short sarcastic speech.

"I thank you all for coming, you see the deceased my father is somewhere in hell getting burnt and I'd like to show you all what is happening to his body right now," he lit a fire and set the body ablaze. My sisters screamed and oh words cannot describe the scene, we all helplessly watched as our dad's body was cremated. My sisters wept their eyes out, they wanted to tear Dele Martins apart but they were firmly held by their husbands. I'm sure you're wondering what happened to my mum? After the revelation, she fell into a coma and was rushed to the hospital. I hated her with such an intensity that I could not describe. All I could think of was squeezing life out of her body, how could she be so unfaithful to a point of not knowing the father of her own child! Happy was three years older than Dele Martins indicating that my righteous father was also unfaithful...

How was I ever going to trust anyone in my life? I contemplated suicide but the thought of my wife and two children held me back. I started having doubts about my own children, was it possible that Tessy too was seeing someone else? I decided to take my children for blood test to truly ascertain their paternity but I dismissed the thought. It was no use but the discovery brought me to a realization that women are evil. The greatest sin a woman would commit against her husband is adultery as it could lead to a man becoming a father to children that are not his. My next plight was to find out who my father was and I had to do so by meeting my mum even though I had no desire to set my eyes on her for the rest of my life. I entered her room and closed the door behind me; she could not look at me in the eye.

"Tom I am very sorry, I don't know what to say to you"

"Just tell me who my father is, I want to know him" I replied

"Your father is Doctor Kolade"

"Dr Kolade?"

"Yes, you still remember him right? He is the doctor that treated you when you were depressed"

"I damn well know him, so that's my dad? But mummy, are you sure? Was he the only doctor that was screwing you?"

"Tom I deserve to be insulted but I crave your understanding… he is the only person I had an extramarital affair with"

"I hope you are saying the truth dear mother… where is my dear father?"

"Right now he's out of the country to receive some kind of treatment"

"Where exactly is he?" I yelled at her.

"He went to Spain, look Tom you were conceived out of love, Dr. Kolade and I have been in love ever since I set my feet into the hospital but we could do nothing about it because he was happily married and so was I… as it appeared to the whole world anyway… he will be very happy and pleased if he realizes that you are his son. We always thought of having a baby together but we always took precautions, as we never had the courage to carry out such an act. I had no idea that you were his son… Tom say something, don't just stand there staring at me…"

What was I supposed to say to all the trash she was telling me?

"What do you want me to say mum except to thank you very much for making me live a lie, thank you very much I'm grateful" she started weeping

"Oh Tom, please forgive me, I pray you never experience the kind of Passion that consumed Dr. Kolade and I…it was so strong yet so deadly. Flesh is useless Tom, we tried but could not resist. Our passion for each other had to die a long time ago. We actually murdered it because it wanted to consume us, never did I know that the ghost of passion would rise to torment me… all I expect from you right now is forgiveness, please forgive me Tom. Your father has no right at all to cut you out of his will, he also experienced such an emotion with Dele's mum so he knows what it feels like. Do you know what it feels like? I pray you never get into such a destructive emotion. Being without Dr. Kolade was torture. He made me happy… he made blood flow through my veins…"

"What of daddy? You mean you didn't love him?"

"I loved your dad…but I realized I married the wrong person immediately I met Dr. Kolade. There are different types of love. Ours was a passionate kind of love that transcends all human understanding, you are just an unfortunate but innocent victim of my unfaithfulness, all I have I shall leave for you, you are my only heir…." she kept crying, I felt like consoling her by gathering her into my arms and pleading with her not to worry but I could not, after taking two steps towards her, I backed out and rushed out of the house, I went somewhere quiet where I poured out my heart by crying. As the tears cascaded, I knew that I was going to be all right. Funny enough I didn't even have the urge to drink as usual, alcohol my earthly comforter could not help me out of a burden as heavy as this. All I could think of was what used to be. I admired nature, the carefree birds of the air, the air itself so invisible yet so indispensable. The sea, so gentle and calm right now but could get very violent during a storm. Later I went back home feeling very refreshed but to receive a sad news, my mum committed suicide! What a period of deaths. Her burial was quiet as everyone was already drained of all emotions.

My next problem was seeing my dad, locating his house was not a problem I went to the hospital and before you could blink your eyes I got his address. I started having second thoughts about going to his house when I thought of his wife and children who would definitely become heartbroken if they ever discovered me. Would the children accept me as their brother? For these reasons I decided not to go to his house but I had to go to his house when I discovered that he was not going to go back to work in the hospital as he had resigned.

Mrs. Kolade turned out to be a very beautiful and gentle woman. I was surprised that someone would cheat on a charming lady like her because she was much more beautiful than my mum. She ushered me in and asked me to sit down, then she brought me a drink. I don't know if her hospitality was borne out of loneliness or if it was her normal nature to be so good to strangers.

"I'm so sorry that you have to see him desperately and I cannot help you, I feel sad when someone needs something and I can't give it to him" I smiled at her in reply.

I asked for her album just to get to see what my family looked like. I went through to discover that I looked like some of the children, which was a great shock to me, and I started weeping she saw the tears in my eyes.

"Why are you crying?"

"What did you say ma"

"Why are you crying?"

"I have a little problem with my eyes tears keep oozing out of it"

"Sorry, is that why you want to see my husband?"

"Its one of the reasons wow, you have such lovely children" she introduced her children one after the other; they were four in all three sons and a daughter. Afterwards she brought a bigger album, which contained all her grandchildren. Then she brought the smallest album and showed me her great grandchildren, just four of them.

"Wow, that's a nice collection you have there"

"There's something I'll tell you that will shock you"

"What?" I asked

"I took all those photographs myself"

"You don't say"

"Yes, I took the pictures myself, photography has always been my hobby. When I retired from work I went into it full time with my family as my sole customers"

"You mean they pay you?"

"Of course"

"There's something else that will shock you"

"Oh, what?" I asked

"I have video tapes of all my children from birth till date"

"Wow that is lovely"

"Would you like to see the tapes?"

"I would have loved to but, it would take some time and I have to go right now..."

"Come on boy, you don't have to watch everything, at least 4 tapes on each child,"

"4 tapes!" I exclaimed

"Come on dear, I know that you won't want to stop once you start watching" I stayed for two reasons, firstly, I didn't want to make an old woman feel sad and secondly because I wanted to see my brothers and sisters. I finally left the house at about eleven p.m. She asked me to come back a week later to see her husband.

"But you could discuss anything with me and I'll get it across to him"

"This is so serious that I must discuss it with him alone"

"All right, if you say so, but I can assure you that we have no secret from each other, telling me would be as good as telling him" I smiled and said goodnight to her. I felt pity for her because she believed in her husband so much. How would she feel if she ever discovers that he was cheating on her all these years? In any case my discussion with Dr. Kolade could never hold, as he didn't make it back from his journey. He kicked the bucket on his way back into the country. I felt terrible when I heard the news but what could I do? To continue with life was the only thing that I could do but it was so pathetic that I ended up not really getting to know my dad. All I knew about him was that I was once his patient and he was so nice to me…

"Tom don't worry at least we had an encounter with him and he was so nice to us" Tessy said when we got back from his burial.

"Tessy I wish I got the opportunity of meeting him again. Do you know that sometimes I long to spend time with him but at same time I hate him because he made me lose my inheritance, everything would have been shared between Dele and I"

"Tom, forget all that. God knows why he allowed it. Always think positively about your dad, he was such a charming man and he made sure I promised him that I was going to take care of you and never leave you till eternity. He told me that you loved me so much and went ahead to differentiate between being in love and showing love"

"Tess, He thought me how to show a woman love, he actually told me about how his blood boiled for my mum"

"He did?"

"Yes, but I didn't even think it could be my mum. I actually imagined a young damsel"

"Come on Tom, I see your dad as a very open person that exudes love, please think no evil of him"

"Yes, my dad was a very passionate person but what I don't understand is why he didn't love his wife"

"Who says he does not love his wife?"

"Would he be cheating on her if he loved her?"

Chapter 23

EVERYTHING CHANGED, NOTHING was the same anymore, I did not feel like the same person anymore.

I resumed work to find out that everything had changed as well. Dele Martins had assumed his position without even waiting for a proper handover. I can't still understand why Dele hated me so much; he got everything yet he made sure that I lost the little I had.

Believe me, I never had more than one bank account. I never really bothered about money, it was just there all the time that you would not think of keeping money in different banks. My account was frozen by Dele, which left me with no money of my own. I guess that's one of the numerous mistakes I made in my life.

All the money I had was what my mum left for me and the raw cash I had at home.

Dele sacked me from work; it wasn't as if I wanted to continue working there anyway. All I left the office with was my credentials and car, as I was not paid any severance nor gratuity. My sisters entered a fierce battle with Dele to get back my job but I was no longer interested.

I became pissed off with life. A frustrated man would certainly not be good company for anybody especially my wife whom I could not help but vent all my anger and frustrations upon.

I entered the labor market totally oblivious of how competitive it was. I wrote lots of applications but no job ever came up. Mac's dad wanted me to work for him but I turned down the offer, because, I realized that all my life I had been fed with silver spoons, which got me nowhere. I decided to try eating with other type of spoons especially the plastic types.

I wanted to do everything on my own without using any of my numerous 'connections' Life was really not a bed of roses. I tried my entire best not to commit suicide. It wasn't as if I had no money, my sisters kept giving me money my wife was also working and supporting the family. But all these monies were never enough for the family. One cool evening, after dinner Mr. Alexander came to see me

"Tom I was instructed by your dad to give you this letter six months after his burial"

"Thanks…" I took the letter to my quiet balcony and sat down there to read and digest the contents.

My dear son,

I know you are surprised reading from me. I know you are also surprised that I am still calling you my son. Please don't be because you are truly the only son I had in my life. Be faithful to your wife. This son of mine Dele Martins Davies was a mistake because of my infidelity. My punishment for such an act is that my company must die! Yes the company will die because Dele will not allow it live. He will destroy all that we labored for because he does not have what you have and what you have is what the company needs to survive. I didn't live anything for you because I know Dele will fight you besides I know that your real

father will leave you an inheritance. Dele hates you so much, I
don't know why so be wary of him. You will be a great man and
God will bless you immensely. Please forgive me for the way I
treated you. I didn't know how to go about everything. But I was
so sure that I would break down and tell you everything if I ever
looked into your eyes hence I decided to keep a distance between
us. Tom I love you so much, much more than any living soul…
I was not happy when you got married because I wanted to die
before you got married then the whole truth would have come
out and you would have been more cautious about who to marry.
Not as if I have anything against your wife, she is very pretty and
I pray that God will bless your marriage. Even in my grave I shall
continue to watch over you. Don't ever forget the time we spent
together… Your children shall make you a proud father because
you made me a proud father.

You shall live long and not die in shame like me.

I have so much to say but don't know how.

Are you crying? I wrote this letter in tears as well.

I wish you a happy life but to achieve this eschew sin because
the devil is always looking for whom to devour. I miss you so
much.

I cried like a baby after reading the letter. I felt his presence
so much, as though his spirit was right beside me also shedding
tears. I closed my eyes and suddenly we were together again… he
was wiping away my tears and I was wiping away his. I told him
I was not angry with him anymore, he smiled at me and thanked
me, then we hugged each other so tightly…and cried more…

"Daddy I am so alone I want to be with you like this forever"

"Me too, but we belong to different worlds now all the time we
were destined to share we have shared…"

"It hurts me so much that we spent the last years miles apart"

"Me too"

"Why did the devil tear us apart? Daddy why did the devil
destroy our happiness?"

"Not the devil my son, the ghost of passion, deadlier than the
devil destroyed us…" Tessy tapped me

"Tom you are hallucinating!"

"No I was with my dad, see the letter he gave me"

"Hey it was the lawyer that brought it and not your dad, come on lets go to bed" she dragged me up and I followed her into the house with anger. Why the hell did she stop my conversation with my dad?

"Tessy I was enjoying myself, I was with my dad today after such a long time and he apologized for all his wrong doing"

"Don't worry my love, you are going to enjoy yourself even better because I'm going to make passionate love to you" she said closing the door behind her, my head started spinning as she mentioned passion, the deadly ghost of passion that threw daddy and I apart....

"No Tess I don't want you to make it passionate, passion has a deadly ghost its better you just make love to me because I hate passion, daddy told me what it caused, mummy also said the same thing..."

"Will you just keep quiet" she whispered as we walked past the children's room. We entered our room and she started taking off her clothes smiling at me. I felt like running away, she was about to unleash passion upon me and I didn't want that... then she walked up to me and started kissing me... 'the ghost of passion deadlier than the devil...' was all I could hear. I pushed Tessy away and screamed

"Daddy please come and help me..." that was how the climax of my catastrophe occurred. I woke up the next day to find myself in a psychiatric hospital! I had gone nuts. I responded to treatment pretty well and was discharged after four months. I was cured of schizophrenia but not of erectile dysfunction. I became impotent. Tessy could never forgive me for it, as if it was my doing, I tried working on my mind and also took various drugs but it kept failing me so I stopped, Pfizer pharmaceuticals had not discovered Viagra at that time. I expected Tessy to understand but she never could and that was the beginning of things falling apart between tessy and I.

Chapter 24

I DON'T KNOW ABOUT you, but what makes me feel good when I think of going home is not really seeing my wife and children, yes seeing them gives me Joy but what makes me really satisfied is entering my house, my home a place of my own. What makes a home? You would wonder, what made my home were my wife, children, memories and every piece of furniture in my house.

Whenever I enter my house and see my children's toys scattered all over the place, I feel happy.

Whenever I walk through the doors of my house and behold the beautiful angelic painting my mother gave me on my tenth birthday I feel happy.

Whenever I enter my children's room and see how a plain room was transformed into a nursery with wallpaper, on which was drawn teddy bears, I feel happy.

Whenever I enter the kitchen and see that tiny wall clock we were given at our favourite grocery store I feel happy. It was a big argument between Tessy and I about where to keep it. I wanted it in my car while Tessy wanted it in the kitchen, she won at the end and we kept it in the kitchen. That tiny clock shaped like an apple gave me joy whenever I glanced at it.

Another thing that made my home was the memories created therein.

The most terrible calamity occurred one Friday evening. I call it a calamity because all I built bit by bit was lost in a few hours; my lovely house was consumed by a mysterious fire accident! Everything was burnt to ashes. We had to move to the family house that is Chioma's house who was very pleased to have us. I guess she is the only true mother I ever had. There was no possible way of ever replacing everything. Part of our lives had been burnt, taken away from us forever. Tessy tried her best to adjust but later she could not bear it any more.

One evening as we were about to go to bed, Tessy suggested we see Dele martins and plead with him to give me back my Job. I was very annoyed with her suggestion.

"Tessy how could you ever suggest something as stupid as that, you know that Dele Martins hates me very much. He took away my Job, burnt my house..."

"Come off that Tom, you can't say that Dele burnt the house"

"Then who burnt the house?"

"How do you expect me to have an answer to that? Any way, it's humiliating asking for money from your sisters and accepting money from Mac, you need your Job back"

"Look here Tessy, my sisters give us money from the depth of their heart and they always try to give us more than enough. All we have to do is to cut down on our expenses, let's spend wisely."

"Are you saying that I am not spending wisely?"

"No don't quote me wrongly, I said 'we' not 'you'"

"Tom you are really enjoying this right? Just sitting down seeing the children and I suffer brings you pleasure. All you have to do is to get off your high horse and face reality. Dele just wants to humble you"

"Humble? What do you mean? Tessy you mean I am not humble?"

"Tom, if you were humble you would have gone to plead with Dele, you need his help, we all do"

I stood up and walked out on her, before I would say something that we both would regret. The next morning, I left the house very early for Ibadan to get new credentials as all my documents got burnt in the fire accident.

To my greatest shock, there was no trace of me in the school, no file, nothing in my Department to prove that I was once a student of that University. The first thing that came to my mind was Dele Martins. I realized the intensity of Dele's hatred for me as I was convinced in my heart that Dele was responsible, just like the fire accident. I traveled back home dejected. I went straight to Mac's house and told him everything. Mac could not believe it He said he was going to confront him the next day. Mac and Yvonne cheered me up as usual. When I got home, I ran straight to bed. The next morning, Tessy woke me up with breakfast in bed. I told her about my credentials, she was surprised but she dismissed the fact that, Dele could be behind it. Looking for a job had to come to a stand still as I had to start searching for my credentials.

Mac accused Dele martins but he denied all allegations. The investigators we sent to Ibadan searched and searched the whole school but there was not tiny proof that could show that I graduated from the school. I became a frustrated man. My wife came home with money one evening

"Tom I went to see Dele Martins and he gave me some money"

"He gave you money?"

"Yes", she replied", I asked and I was given, He didn't even question me, he sends his regards"

"Nonsense, Tessy how could you do such a thing without consulting me?"

"I knew you were not going to accept it. Tom I had to pay the children's school fees and I dare not go to Mac, Yvonne or Happy, because they sent us a hundred and fifty thousand naira last week"

"What happened to the money?"

"It got finished"

"How can you finish a hundred and fifty thousand naira in one week without paying the children's school fees?"

"I had to buy foodstuffs, some clothes and other things that the family needed".

"Tessy between clothes and school fees which is more important?"

"Do you expect me to wear rags to work?"

"Not really, all I expected is for you to manage the ones you have for now until..."

"Until what Tom? Until when? You don't have a job, you are not even expecting one soon..."

"I see someone has lost faith in me"

"It's not as if I've lost faith in you but please let's face the stark reality"

"And what is the stark reality? I guess the reality here is that I'm doomed for life right?"

"I am not saying that, anyway I told Dele that we were starting a business center and he gave me this five hundred thousand naira for a start, he explained the reasons why he sacked you to me, Tom Dele has a good heart"

"Oh my God, I can't believe I'm hearing this, Tessy what about our house that got burnt and my certificates that disappeared?"

"Tom he is not behind any ill luck that has befallen us, he swore by his father's grave" I busted out laughing.

"Look at you Tessy you believed that fool, have you forgotten that his father has no grave?"

"Tom whatever you say, I've decided to look at the bright side of Dele. He has a good heart..."

"Tessy what about my certificates, I accept Dele has nothing to do with the fire but how did all my files disappear from school? Who on earth would do something like that to me?"

"I don't have an answer to that. Tomorrow I'm going to shop for computers after paying the children's school fees"

"No you are not, you are going to return the money tomorrow okay?"

"Not okay Tom, I am not returning the money"

She had pushed me to the wall; I pounced on her and gave her the beating of her life. Her screams woke the whole family, Chioma and the children rushed to our room but they could not come in because it was locked.

Our kids were crying and Chioma was shouting out to me to stop but I didn't. I stopped when I was really tired and she was screaming no more. I took my car keys and left the house.

I came back by midnight; Chioma was waiting up for me.

"Thomas I know what you're going through, things have not been easy for you but I assure you that you are just going through trials"

"Chioma, how could she go and ask for money from someone that wants to destroy me"

"I understand but she did it in the interest of the family. It's not easy for someone to cut down on his expenses. She's used to being extravagant and it will take time..."

"Just last week we got one hundred and fifty thousand and she blew everything, how could she spend a hundred and fifty thousand without paying the children's school fees?"

"Tom please, learn to settle things with your wife, you do not understand her. When was the last time you sent her family money?"

"Chioma I honestly have not sent them anything since after the wedding"

"You see Tom she told me about the state of things in her family. Out of the one hundred and fifty thousand she sent eighty thousand home because her auntie had been hospitalized and she needed to settle the hospital bills.

"But, she never mentioned it, how was I supposed to know... Damn!"

"Tom you find out by asking. You should constantly ask after your in-laws to find out how they are faring, Tom you've not been caring, you've been neglecting your wife completely"

I felt really ashamed of myself. How was I ever going to make it up to her? I knew it was going to be difficult, I knew I would never accept Dele's money and I was sure that she would not want to return the money. Making up was going to be really difficult.

I thanked Chioma and went to bed in the guestroom.

The next morning I stayed in my room because I did not want to run into Tessy till she left for work.

Chioma brought breakfast for me in my room and informed me that my wife was seriously Ill so I rushed up to see her. There were bruises all over her face, I had no idea the magnitude of injuries I had inflicted on her. I called Yvonne to come to my rescue. She was really angry with me. I told her what happened but she would not reason with me.

"Listen to me Tom" Yvonne said, "no matter what she did to you, you have no rights whatsoever to beat her up like a goat" I asked Yvonne to return Dele's money and she accepted.

When Tessy opened her eyes she found herself in a place as beautiful as paradise. I decorated her room with bright flowers. Red roses, cards everywhere-get well wishes, love declarations as well as apology cards.

I made sure that I was always there for her, just like when she was pregnant for our first baby, I stayed with her until all the bones I had broken in her body became fused again.

When Tessy became very well and started moving around, I pleaded with her to forgive me and she accepted my apologies, she told me that she deserved all I did to her but I would not hear of it.

"No Tessy I was the one that went wrong"

"Come on Tom, I went wrong"

"No Tess I did"

"Tom you know that I am the guilty party?

"Guilty? Tessy, guilt is what is killing me".

"I'm the one dying of guilt Tom"

"No you are not"

"Yes I am…"

Then we both started laughing, it was so funny arguing over nothing. We decided to put the incident right behind us. We became a happy family once more. But wait minute does happiness last forever?

Chapter 25

L IFE THEY SAY is a general drama of pain in which happiness is nothing but an episode in this general drama of pain.

But of course the episode of happiness in the general drama of pain could last long or even forever if we stopped fussing and start viewing our situations differently.

My feelings of worthlessness stopped as I started viewing my situation differently and also Tessy stopped complaining about money. Investigations were still being carried out about the where about of my certificates.

All I did each day was to take the children to school, go back home, surf the Internet, then I'll go get my kids from school in the afternoon, we would have lunch and I'll help them with their assignments afterwards. In the evening Tessy would come back, we would spend time with the children, have dinner and take them to bed together, those days our family was a happy one.

One afternoon, I decided to go to the company to visit Mac. I knew it was going to be a surprise because since I left the company I had not set my foot there. As I walked past my office I saw Joy my secretary.

"Hello Joy" I greeted her. She was very excited to see me.

"Mr. Davies, how are you? Long time!"

"I'm fine" I replied.

"I'm sure you came to see your wife"

"My wife?"

"You can go right in, she is with Mr. Martins"

"My wife?"

"Of course" she replied, "isn't she the one you're looking for?"

"Yes, yes I replied, but I'll check Mac first" I slumped on the sofa immediately I entered Mac's office.

Mac was so surprised to see me.

"To what honor do I owe this visit? Tom, I'm so glad to see you"

"Mac how often does Tessy come here?"

"Come where?"

"Does Tessy come to this company often?"

"I don't know Tom; I've never seen her here anyway"

"Mac she's with Dele Martins right now and I went to the parking space to check her car but it was not there"

"What makes you think that she's with Dele when you didn't see her car?"

"Joy told me, the way she said it reveals everything... she's been seeing Dele Martins"

"I can't believe this" Mac said "but Tom give me a minute, I'll be right back"

When Mac came back he was down cast probably because he saw doom about to encroach upon my family, a kind of premonition that the end was going to be doom... I sensed that something was amiss.

"Tom, its true, Tessy is with Dele Martins I'm just from his office"

"Damn that woman" I said.

"Tom, please don't jump into a conclusion they could be discussing business"

"Mac I have to be calm"

"Yes Tom, you are right, you have to be calm"

"I also have to get evidence, Mac I'll have to start trailing her"

"Tom calm down, I am sure she'll tell you everything she came here for immediately she gets home"

"She better does Mac, she better does"

"Tom I am going to ask you for a favour right now and I'm not taking no for an answer"

"What is it?"

"Please don't beat her up again"

Mac saw me off to the car. As I walked past my secretary saw me,

"She is still in there, should I…"

"Yes I know" I replied, "I called her from Mac's office, thank you very much"

"You've not answered me, promise me that you wouldn't beat her up or raise the issue, just pretend that you know nothing let's see what she will do".

"All right Mac, I promise. I don't know what to think or do anymore, I thought we were all happy, I can't believe that she would start misbehaving again"

"Mac, What if they are going out?"

"Don't even think about it, please don't jump into a conclusion, I am sure you will be told everything when she get home"

Tessy came back home and behaved normally. I expected her to talk about her visit to Dele Martins but she said nothing and I didn't ask her, she was sort of nicer than her usual self.

I called Mac the next day and informed him that Tessy didn't tell me anything. We decided that Mac would come to the house that evening perhaps, Tessy will remember they met in Dele's office and tell me what she went there for.

After dinner we sat in the sitting room to chat.

"Tessy how have you been" Mac inquired

"Fine" she replied, "you've refused to visit us but I understand, having two set of twins is not easy"

"How many set of twins does Tom have that he does not visit us?"

"None" I replied.

"You see, Tessy, my kids have nothing to do with this, it's just that I stopped coming because you guys stopped coming. Tessy the other day that at the office you didn't even come to say good-bye" said Mac

"At the office?" Tessy inquired she wanted to deny it.

"Yes, the day I saw you in Dele Martin's office."

"Oh that, sorry I left in a hurry I was late for a meeting" She quickly changed the topic.

"But Tom its bad inviting just Mac for dinner"

"I didn't invite Mac for dinner" I replied

"I came myself, Tom didn't invite me" Mac added.

"Well, next time you're coming, come with the whole family"

"Alright" Mac said, "I guess I'll take my leave now"

"Thank God it's a guess, you can go on guessing Mac" I replied

"Then I will leave now" Mac said and we all laughed. Finally I saw Mac off to his car.

"Mac she's hiding something, why were you not more explicit, like ask her what she was doing there?"

"That's what I expected you to ask her Tom. I was surprised that you just kept quiet"

"All right Mac, I'll ask her this night and I'll call you tomorrow"

"Please ask her Tom, so that your suspicions would not make you go paranoid."

As we were in bed, I asked Tessy the dreaded question.

"Tessy are you sleeping"

"No Tom"

"Can I ask you a question?"

"Of course"

"Tessy what did you go to see Dele Martins for?"

"Why I went to see Dele Martins Tom was because of the business centre I wanted to start, remember he gave me money and you were so angry that you broke my bones and nearly killed me remember that, Tom?" she started crying.

"That's not what I'm talking about Tess, I'm talking about the day that Mac saw you there"

"That was the day that Mac saw me Tom, the day you beat me and broke my bones…" She continued crying and I took her into my arms comforting her, I knew it took her courage and great effort to lie to me, I knew she was crying because she lied to me, but what I wanted to really know was why she was lying.

Chapter 26

I HAD TO START plan B. after dropping the children in school I would Trail Tessy to everywhere she went. I hated myself for doing it but I had to.

I almost got tired of trailing her because nothing came up, then it happened! Tessy came out of her office, and took a taxi. I followed her immediately. The taxi took her to a house, in which she spent two hours. Afterwards She came out took another taxi and went back to her office. I could not believe it, Tessy was not only begging Dele Martins for money, she was also having an affair with him. She was sleeping with Dele Martins, the man who crippled my life.

I went straight to Mac and told him everything. Mac said I had no evidence. Firstly I didn't see the person or people in the house so there was no evidence that Dele Martins was the guy, Secondly there was no evidence that she slept with whomever it was probably they were discussing business.

"Tom please don't get paranoid" Mac concluded.

I tried all my best to keep calm at home, but I still kept a trail on Tessy. a week later she went to the same house at the same time and left after two hours.

I didn't leave immediately this time, I waited a while and Dele Martins finally emerged from the gates in his navigator jeep.

"I knew it" I said to myself. The bitch was meeting Dele Martins every week for 2 hours of whatever. My worst fear had been confirmed and I didn't know what I was going to do about it. Two hours with Dele Martins made my wife a very radiant and happy woman filled up with smiles. It was then I realized that her happiness lied in the arms of Dele Martins.

My self-control was beyond me that night. As we got to the bedroom she wore her sexiest nightgowns. I went straight to the bathroom thinking of how I was going to share a bed with the stupid bitch.

"Tom come here" she said lying down on the bed.

"Tommy come here please," she repeated seductively. I was still suffering from my temporary impotence. I came out of the bathroom.

"Tessy here I am"

"Come here to bed Tom, let's try tonight who knows, you might recover"

"I don't think so"

"Tom we have to keep trying, if we had been trying I'm sure that things would have been normal now"

"But Tessy you had 2 hours of sex today what else do you want or have you suddenly become a nymphomaniac?"

It was as if a bomb dropped, I myself could not believe that I said it, I had no intention of saying it, not tonight because I had not decided what to do about it.

Before, I could realize what I had said Tessy stood up and ran out of the room. I guess she knew that I would have killed her.

The next morning she was off to work before I woke up. She phoned me from her office.

"Yes Tess, what do you want?" I asked

"Tom I am honestly ashamed of myself and understand any decision you take" she replied.

"You see, I have actually not made any decision, maybe you, could tell me what you feel is right"

"Tom I won't mind a divorce, you have never been a loving husband, you do not care about anyone else but yourself, not to talk of how you beat me as if you were beating an animal. Tom I am tired of our marriage, we both know it's not working. I've found true love in Dele... Tom are you there?"

"Of course Tessy, what about the children?" I asked her, "When we get divorced what do we tell them...what will become of them?"

"Don't worry about them Tom I plan to take custody of the children, Dele Martins is willing to have them..."

I burst out laughing hysterically then I hung up on her. It was so funny, Tessy wanted to give my kids to my enemy- Dele Martins.

It shocked me to discover that even when I felt that Tessy was most happy in our marriage, she was actually planning to leave me, what an irony that all the while she was mapping out plans of leaving me. All women are like tea bags I concluded you never know their strength until you drop them in hot water.

Chapter 27

I N ALL MY life, I never thought that I could ever get separated from my wife talk more of get divorced.

I considered myself a very good man that any woman would never leave but how wrong I was. I had my shortcomings but men who treated their wives without any respect still existed and their wives would dare not cheat on them because of their children.

A broken home was never what I bargained for my children. I didn't know what to do, I didn't want the divorce and I also didn't want Tessy in my life anymore. Those were the only two options I had. I was in between the devil and the deep blue sea.

Tessy didn't keep it a secret any longer she would come to the house any time, sometimes she would not even come at all. But I kept my children away from all what was happening always telling them one lie or the other to cover up for her.

Yvonne and Mac could not understand Tessy's behaviour. They both felt so sorry for me so they decided to take the children to their place till things settled between the two of us. No one said anything but we all knew that there was going to be no settlement. My marriage was over. I felt sorry for my two children and terribly missed them. That evening Tessy phoned me, she was still afraid of facing me.

"Tom what happened to the children they are not in bed"

"Where were you yesterday? It didn't occur to you that you had children right?"

"Where are my children?" she demanded sternly

"You really want to know? Why don't you come upstairs and find out" I replied and hung up. She could not come upstairs of course. The next morning she dropped a note telling me that she would pack out of the house

"Tom since the children are no longer staying in this house, there's no use of me staying so I guess its best I pack out. Please I'll like you to leave the house at about five p.m. to seven p.m. Thanks"

As I was not a monster I stayed in the house. I even offered to help her pack. Chioma wept, she begged Tessy and I to reconsider but Tessy turned deaf ears. I honestly didn't feel sad but I was not happy either just numb. Who was I to deny her of her new found happiness? She was surprised at my behaviour

"I'll send my lawyer" she said when she got into her car. "Please I'll like you to be rational about the children"

"Alright" I replied, "I'll be waiting" she was reluctant to start the car.

"Tom I'm really sorry for leaving you in this way believe me it was not intentional" I stared at her without a word.

"Tom, I honestly don't know what to say to you?"

"I don't know what to say either I wish you a good life"

"So do I, bye Tom"

"Bye Tess"

Then she drove out of the house. I stood there for about fifteen minutes looking into space before Chioma come to usher me in. I cried uncontrollably like a baby, Chioma consoled me till I fell asleep right there in the sitting room. Chioma woke me up at about 9pm for dinner. We went to the dining area to eat. I could not help but reminiscence about the past.

I recalled how my dad, mum, happy and I used to have our meals.
Later it became my dad, my mum, Yvonne, happy and I.
Happy left and it was just my dad, my mum, Yvonne and I.
Then my dad fell ill and it was just Yvonne, my mum and I
Then Yvonne got married and it was just my mum and I.
Then I got married and it was just Chioma and my mum.
Then my mum died and Chioma was left alone.
Then it was Chioma, Tessy, our kids and I.
Then it became Chioma, the Kids and I.
And now it's just Chioma and I.

Wow, how things change. I wondered who the next family that
would sit on this dining table to eat would be. We heard a knock
on the door. To my greatest shock I saw Dele Martins right in
front of my doorstep! What did he want this time? I noticed that
his eyes were bloodshot.

"Can I come in please?" he inquired.

"I don't think so" I replied, "What do you want"

"I want to discuss something with you"

"Look Dele or whatever you call yourself, if it's my wife, you
can have her, I've realized that anything I have, you always go
after. Now tell me why would a fine man like you like leftovers
so much?"

"Tom please listen to me"

"There's nothing we have to say to each other, you've burnt my
house, destroyed my certificates and files, you've taken my wife_...
Dele you've ruined me isn't that enough for you?"

"Tom I honestly love your wife we were made for each other
but..."

"Look Dele, I'm not going to stay here and listen to you, you
love her and you've got her, so please both of you stay out of my
life" and I closed the door. The doorbell rang again and I opened
the door angrily.

"Dele get out of here before I do something nasty to you"

"Tom, I came to tell you that Tessy is dead"

"What?" I shouted.

"Tessy is dead Tom"

Chapter 28

THAT WAS HOW Tessy ended up, death was what drove her out of my life, death was what she found in the arms of Dele Martins, Death wanted Tessy and it sure did get her. Perhaps she would have not been discovered by death had she not left me. The ghastly motor accident, which occurred right in front of Dele Martins residence, claimed her life despite all attempts by the doctors to save her. At least she died in the arms of lover boy who was with her as she struggled to overcome death.

Our children cried so much when I explained to them that they would never see their mum again. After their mum's burial, Mac and Yvonne took my children.

I continued staying with Chioma but all I could do was reminiscence about the past. Was this how I was going to spend the rest of my life?

I decided to go somewhere far away where I would start all over again. A new identity, a new hair cut... that was how I left my first world and walked into another world, a world I ought to have been right from the start.

Right now its fifty-five years since I left but it feels just like yesterday.

Beginning a new life was not easy during the first few months, I kept feeling like talking to somebody from home, at least talking to Mac alone but I resisted the urge because in my note I told them to forget about me, I know that the note would have broken their hearts.

Dear Mac and Yvonne,

What do I say to you two? Yvonne you are my sister but all my life you've cared about me like a mother and now my children you've taken as your own. Yvonne what can I say to you except that I love you and appreciate all you've done for me. Mac you were like a father to me all my life and I have no doubt that you'll be a good father to my children too. The union of you both was truly ordained by God. As my children are in the best hands, I have to do something with the remaining of my life. I can't take the heat anymore. Immediately I settle down, I'll get in touch with you. Say goodbye to Happy and the boys for me. It's as if I should not go but I have to be strong, I'll miss you all, two of you especially but I guess the memories of you that I have in my heart would compensate for the loss. Goodbye and thanks.

Thomas.

My dreams finally came to a reality. I became an engineer! Not a real engineer anyway but a mechanic. Being an apprentice was not a bed of roses. I had a space to sleep at nights in the garage at least that stopped me from roaming the streets.

My life as an apprentice was far more interesting than my life in the University. The garage was a learning institution in which I took my studies with utmost seriousness that within two years I was an expert. My master was so impressed with my expertise that he employed me. Within a few years I opened my own garage and got married to a beautiful lady. She was the daughter of the food seller at the garage. Those days when I had no money, she would send me food whenever her mum was away. She loved me with all her heart and that was why I married her when I became a 'somebody'- the most intelligent mechanic in that city. I went into my second marriage because of the love and respect my wife had for me. My business expanded, we had children and sent them to the best schools. Believe me there's nothing as joyous as earning your own money, starting from the scratch without anyone's help. Now my wife's gone, my children have all settled down and my grandchildren are also coming up. I feel I've lived a lie as even my wife died without knowing about my past. Now I'm ready to let the cat out of the bag but no one wants to believe me. I don't know what to do but I sure do feel lighter now, as the burden of deception has been lifted from my shoulders.

In my lifetime the greatest asset I ever had was my breath of life, yes being alive gave me the opportunity to fulfill my destiny. The saying that when there's life there's hope is a truism any day and he who gives life God Almighty, is the greatest of all.

About the Author

HABIBAT ONYIOZA SHEIDU an African from Nigeria was born on the 28th of November 1979. She started writing at a very tender age and was a member of various press clubs from primary school through university where she became the first female editor in chief of the Pharmasearch magazine. Habibat has travelled the world studying across disciplines, as well as working and living with people from diverse cultures. She uses seamlessly yet intricately her knowledge of people, science, arts and social sciences in her writing in a manner that inspires imagination, provokes learning and captivates the reader. Habibat enjoys travelling and writing. Ghost of Passion is her first novel.

Printed in the United States
By Bookmasters